QUEERLEADERS

About the Author

When M.B. isn't writing, they work as a producer of the theatrical trailers everyone talks through when they go to the movies. They also spend their spare time skating in roller derby, pretending they are a cowboy and playing with swords. Living in Los Angeles with their partner and herd of fur children has taught them useful defensive driving skills and how to avoid celebrities. They have kindly requested that, if the time ever comes, their lifeless corpse be dragged into LA County limits before they are officially declared dead.

QUEERLEADERS

M.B. GUEL

BELLA
BOOKS
2020

First Bella Books Edition 2020

Editor: Ann Roberts
Cover Designer: Ally Baldwin

ISBN: 978-1-64247-115-1

Acknowledgements

Thank you to my wife, Ally, for putting up with me staring uselessly at a computer for hours while I "wrote". Thank you to Lucky for being the best idea bouncer/beta/possum I could ask for. Last but not least, thanks to the Little Shit Show that dragged me back into writing and the wonderful humans who helped get me here.

Dedication

To my 5th grade teacher who tried to give me an F on my book report because it was "written too well for a ten-year-old."

CHAPTER ONE

The dull thunder of rubber balls bouncing off the hardwood floor in the gym might as well have been torture. The familiar scent of old sports equipment intermingled with the feet of pubescent teenagers permeated the air. This was Mack's personal version of hell.

Mack jumped away as a bright red ball whizzed past her head. She wasn't quite sure why dodgeball was even legal. It was basically a form of child abuse, giving a bunch of hormonal, angst-ridden teenagers dodgeballs and permission to hurl them at each other. They were basically pitting students against students in a fight to the death. It was primitive.

Mack risked a glance at the clock. Forty-nine minutes of PE remained. Time seemed to roll backward in this horrific universe.

She plucked at the baggy T-shirt hanging around her lanky frame. Mack avoided looking at herself in the mirror as much as possible. How many times did she have to see boring short brown hair, pale, almost fluorescent skin and awkwardly long limbs looking back at her? She hadn't even inherited her mom and dad's tanned skin. Puberty, in her opinion, had not been kind, though she thought at seventeen she was supposed to be growing out of her awkward phase already.

Looking down at the too-big basketball shorts, which shapelessly graced her lower half, she turned to Lila beside her. Somehow she had managed to avoid being hit with any of the dodgeballs, despite the fact that she was occupied with picking polish off her nails. Mack considered her with a resigned sigh. Lila seemed to avoid the awkward teenage phase altogether. In the summer between sophomore and junior year, she got the boobs and curves most girls dreamed about.

If she hadn't been her best friend for years, Mack might have resented her.

"I just don't get why these uniforms are so small," Mack complained, tightening her ponytail. "How do they expect us to do any sort of physical activity if we're worried about flashing everyone?"

Lila brushed her raven-colored hair across her shoulder and rolled her neck to look at Mack, giving her a onceover with her eyes.

"You realize you bought yours two sizes too big, right?"

Mack turned to Lila whose uniform was significantly tighter, her tanned skin completely on display. Mack scoffed in offense, "This is the appropriate size, Lila."

Lila just shrugged and went back to disinterestedly picking at her cuticles, not even flinching as another ball flew past her.

"Are we going to the football game tonight?" Mack asked, trying to appear casual.

"Why? So you can stare at the cheerleaders? I don't see you complaining about their uniforms being too tight."

"Mackenzie! Lila! Participate!" the balding gym teacher yelled from his spot on the bleachers.

Mack picked up a ball and threw it halfheartedly. It arched high in the air and fell nowhere near anyone on the other team.

"Why don't you just stare at them now so we don't have to go to the stupid game," Lila said, gesturing to the cheerleaders in the opposite corner of the gym.

"I don't stare. I just appreciate the art of their sport," Mack insisted. She aimed to kick a ball as it rolled toward her, but it hit the side of her foot and spun away from her pathetically.

Lila chuckled. "Sure. Perv."

Mack snuck a look over her shoulder at the cheerleaders just as Veronica took her place at the top of the pyramid. It was very much like a cheesy romance film in Mack's mind. Time seemed to slow as Veronica swung her long, blond ponytail over her shoulder, pompoms high in the air. All the noise in the gym faded away and she was sure there were harps playing somewhere in the distance. Mack swore that Veronica looked right at her and winked as she was being tossed into the air, the dingy gym fluorescent lights somehow making a halo around her airborne form. She went from the cute girl on the playground in preschool to the quintessential pretty blond cheerleader. But she was so much more.

Mack knew she got good grades; she was in all the AP classes and on the Honors List. Sure, she came off as bitchy and self-centered, but someone that pretty and smart couldn't be all that bad. Mack was convinced she was the softest, sweetest girl in school and no one could tell Mack otherwise. Lila wasn't sold on the idea, but Mack pointed out that Veronica had a different puppy calendar in her locker every year. If that didn't say soft, Mack didn't know what did.

Lila sighed. "I miss when you had a crush on that girl at the animal shelter."

"In fifth grade?"

"Yeah. At least she was a good person."

"Coming from the person who hasn't had a boyfriend since kindergarten."

Lila gasped, a dramatic hand to her chest. "I told you. I'm *choosing* to be single."

"For twelve years?"

"I need to focus more on myself, whereas you're just focusing on your weirdo crush for *Veronica*."

"It's not weird."

The last time Mack had spoken to Veronica was the year before. She was in math class and somehow had forgotten to pack a single pencil in her backpack. Veronica sat in front of her, so Mack tapped her shoulder and asked to borrow a pencil. When Veronica leaned back to loan her the pencil, Mack could smell her shampoo from her seat. Plumerias.

When Mack tried to give Veronica the pencil back, she told her to keep it. Mack had the pencil until a few months later when Lila threw it in a sewer. She had been complaining about Mack treasuring the thing. So what if she kept it in a separate pocket of her backpack and carefully sharpened it only just enough? Mack told Lila she was jealous and they didn't talk for a whole period.

Mack couldn't even smell plumerias anymore without blushing.

Suddenly, there was a sharp pain in the side of her head and she snapped back into reality, falling sideways, her body crumpled to the ground. There was a ringing in her ears and she clutched the side of her head, tears of pain pooling at the corners of her eyes. Lila stood over her, hands on her knees as she leaned down.

She shook her head, smug smirk on her face as she repeated. "Total. Perv."

Luckily the teacher blew his whistle, signaling for them to go back to the locker room. Mack changed quickly and got an ice pack for her head that she made a dramatic show of holding as she and Lila walked in the halls.

"You could have warned me!" Mack said as she held the ice pack to her head.

"It's not my fault you were too busy scamming on the bitchiest girl in school to see a ball flying at your face." Lila paused and added, "Oh, the irony."

Mack rolled her eyes. "You're not funny."

In the thirteen years Mack had known Lila, she was always finding a new way to embarrass her. Maybe that's just what happened when you've known someone since you were five years old.

That was pretty much how their entire relationship had worked since then. Lila was everything that Mack needed, even if she denied it most of the time. She was always trying to get Mack to come out of her shell and experience new things. Sometimes it worked, while other times Mack wondered why they were still friends.

Then she remembered there was no one else she'd rather navigate the choppy waters of high school with. They made it through middle school, so they could make it through this. And they had for the most part. It was the home stretch. Only a few more months until graduation and then Mack didn't have to see any of the people she called her classmates ever again, except when she went to the grocery store or the mall...

"I'm pretty funny," Lila said as they turned the hall corner toward their lockers, interrupting Mack's thoughts. "Or else you wouldn't have stuck around with me for so long."

Chad, the typical beefy jock who looked as dumb as he was handsome, hit Mack in the shoulder with his arm as he passed her.

"Watch where you're going, loser." Just the perfect amount of blond hair fell into his eyes. It made Mack want to roll hers.

"Eat a spicy dick!" Lila said, walking backward so she could flip him off with both hands. Chad just flipped her off right back and kept walking to his own locker. Mack actually did roll her eyes this time as she spun the dial on her locker.

"He is such a tool," she muttered.

Lila nodded. "Him and his girlfriend."

Mack blushed and chanced a look back over at Chad who was looking back for some reason, even though Veronica was standing next to him and clearly talking about whatever hot cheerleaders talked about.

"I'm telling you, Lila, there's more to Ronnie than you know," Mack said dreamily.

"Then just tell her if you love her so much."

Mack gasped dramatically and frowned at her friend. "You know I can't do that. I'm not ready for the school to have an opinion on my sex life."

"Or lack thereof," Lila muttered.

Mack smirked. "Does daydreaming about Ronnie count as a sex life?"

Lila pretended to gag and opened her own locker. "You need to get over it. It's pathetic. I just don't even get what you see in her."

"It's hard to explain," Mack said, closing her locker. They began the short walk across the hall toward the classroom and she shrugged. "I'll write you a note. You'll practically be in love with her by the end of it."

"Okay," Lila said skeptically.

They took their seats at the back of the classroom and Mack immediately pulled out a piece of paper. She wrote furiously as she let all her feelings for Veronica come out on paper. She thought about how her nose sloped ever so gently into a little button, her lips…Mack sighed. She was sure that an entire book could be written just about Veronica's lips, or how her blond hair looked like it was spun from gold. She remembered how she smelled like flowers and sunshine. It made Mack's palms sweat just thinking about it.

There was the vague sound of a teacher talking in the background but she couldn't be bothered with it at the moment. She had just put the finishing touches on her letter when the paper was snatched right from under her hands.

Mack looked up quickly, blindly reaching for the paper. Chad looked back at her, paper held high over his head where she couldn't reach it.

"I'm collecting homework, dweeb," he said putting it on top of a pile of papers in his hands.

"You have to give that back," Mack said, her heart in her throat. The last thing she needed was for anyone to get ahold of that note. Especially if that anyone was Chad, the boyfriend of the letter's subject. She felt stupid. Really stupid. She should have known better than to write it down!

"Whatever," he said, walking away as she watched his back helplessly.

"Fuck."

She let her forehead fall on the desk with a thud.

Lila leaned over, trying to get a better look at her friend. "Bro. What's up?"

"I'm dead," Mack groaned. "Chad took the note with the homework." She watched as he handed the pile of papers to the teacher. At least he would never see it.

"Just go ask the teacher for it," Lila said, kicking the leg of Mack's chair. "You need to turn in your real homework anyway. Stop being dramatic."

"You're right," she said, ripping her homework out of her notebook and walking toward the front of the classroom. Mrs. Martinez just stared at her and Mack smiled back nervously. The best way she could describe her was slug-like.

"Heeeeeeeeey," she said in her most casual voice, handing Mrs. Martinez the homework. "Chad accidently picked up a note I had so—"

"You were writing notes in my class?" Mrs. Martinez asked, eyebrows shooting over her glasses.

"No, of course not." Mack offered Mrs. Martinez her best 'obedient student' smile. "I was just…it was a note about how much I loved English."

The teacher blinked at her for a moment and gestured to the pile. "Yeah, fine."

Mack breathed a sigh of relief and began sorting through the pile. "Thank you."

She flipped through each paper, her panic mounting when she couldn't find the note. Her heart stopped as she went through it frantically for the third time.

"It's not here."

"Okay, then sit down please," Mrs. Martinez said, shooing Mack away as she got up for the lecture.

Mack walked back to her desk in a daze, wondering where it would have gone. She leaned over to Lila and whispered, "It wasn't there."

"Where else would it be?" Lila asked just as confused as Mack felt. "You looked all through the homework?"

"Yes," Mack said, looking around the room for even a hint. Everyone seemed invested in their own work and conversations.

"Check the trash cans," Lila whispered.

Mack frowned. "I'm not going to dig through a trash can in the middle of class. Plus they were just emptied."

"That's good, right?"

"Where would it have gone?" Mack whispered back. She looked around the classroom for any sort of clue but only saw Chad looking back at her with a scowl. She rolled her eyes at him and slouched in her seat as she scanned the classroom. Leaning her neck back so she was looking up at the ceiling, Mack felt a sick feeling sinking into her stomach.

CHAPTER TWO

"I don't think you quite understand the gravity of the situation," Mack said as she followed Lila through the crowded cafeteria to their usual spot in the back corner.

"I perfectly understand the gravity of the situation," Lila said, dropping her tray on the table. "There is no gravity to the situation at all."

Mack shot her friend a look. "If anything from that note comes out, I'm ruined."

Lila sat down at the table, Mack across from her, and offered her an amused look. "Here's the thing, Mack," she said, leaning her elbows on the table. "You give yourself a lot of credit. You don't exactly have much to ruin."

Mack barked a humorless laugh. "Of course I do! My perfect disguise of an indifferent heterosexual high schooler who does nothing but drool over prepubescent pop stars could be done for."

"You do that anyhow," Lila said, gesturing wildly with her plastic fork. "Except instead of One Direction, it's Demi Lovato."

Mack pointed her fork at Lila. "Hush! You never know who's listening!"

Lila rolled her eyes. "Listen, you're going to be fine. The note probably ended up in the trash. And if by chance it's still in the homework pile, Mrs. Martinez is just going to toss it."

With a sigh, Mack dropped her fork back on her tray. "You're right," she mumbled. "You're right!"

She leaned back in her chair and looked around the cafeteria. Everyone was minding their own business and entrenched in their own drama. They didn't care about Mack's struggles in the corner. She took a deep breath and tried to let herself be lulled into security. Lila was right. She usually was, a fact the other girl never let Mack forget.

Mack felt eyes on her and looked over her shoulder to see Chad staring at her. Something about the way he was looking at her made Mack shiver. She quickly whipped around back to Lila who was giving her a bored look.

"Chad was staring at me."

Lila raised a skeptical eyebrow and looked over her shoulder. She shrugged and looked back at Mack. "Yeah, I guess you're right."

"That's all you have to say? Do you see how he's looking at me?"

Taking a big bite of her sandwich, Lila looked back toward the football player and cheerleader table.

"Yeah, I guess he always kinda looks at you," Lila said. "Like he's a little bit in love with you."

Mack frowned and shook her head. "What? Okay, no. I can't even touch on that right now," she said, holding a hand up to stop her from talking. "But he looks like he *knows* or something."

"Knows what?"

"I don't know. Maybe he has my note." She gasped in realization. "Oh my god what if he does have my note?"

Lila laughed. "Good one."

"Seriously!"

She glanced back over her shoulder and Chad was still staring, but her eyes caught Veronica next to him. She tossed blond hair over her shoulder, and it caught the light in a way that made Mack feel like she was going to choke. Veronica was talking to Beth, another cheerleader on the squad. Beth had long dark hair that fell in waves over her shoulder, and she was also very pretty, but she never could hold a candle to Veronica. No one could. Beth looked over and caught Mack's eye, waving with a small smile. Veronica caught on and glanced toward Mack, but Mack didn't give herself a chance to see if she'd wave too. She spun back quickly in her seat, eyes wide and on Lila.

"We already decided that Mrs. Martinez has your note," Lila said through another big bite of her sandwich.

As if on cue, Chad climbed on top of the table. The cafeteria hushed and all eyes focused on him.

"I have a bad feeling about this," Mack whispered.

"Don't be so self-centered," Lila said, waving her hand dismissively. "It probably has nothing to do with you."

Chad cleared his throat loudly before he began. "My fellow students, germs and weiners," he boomed. "I have some disturbing news to share with you. It would seem we have a homosexual in our midst."

Mack's whole body stiffened, eyes wide and focused on Lila. Her friend shrugged and tried to remain looking impassive. "Still might not be about you."

"Mack!" Chad said, pointing a finger at her. "I have proof that you're a gay."

It felt like the bottom of Mack's stomach completely fell out. Her palms began to spontaneously sweat.

Lila grimaced at her. "Maybe it is about you."

"You think?" Chad threw a triumphant fist in the air. Clutched in his hand was a piece of paper that Mack knew was hers. With a dramatic flick of his wrist, he unfolded the paper and began to read.

"Hey dumbass, you asked me to list the reasons why I like Veronica, so here it is," Chad said, glancing at Mack before continuing. "Veronica smells like puppies. But not that scent that smells vaguely of piss all the time. It's that soft baby powder smell that they all have for some reason. There's that one time she let me borrow her pencil freshman year, which only proves how sweet she is. She's also really good at cheerleading. It's hard for me to tell but I really do feel more school spirit after she performs…"

The cafeteria had started out suppressing small chuckles, but now they were full on cackling around her. The sound was deafening, drowning out the rest of what Chad was saying, and Mack was sure she had never heard anything worse. Surely, she thought, this was a dream and she'd wake up any moment. She didn't even notice that she had pretty much sunk all the way down in her seat. She looked back at Lila who was frozen mid-bite with half-eaten chicken nuggets on full display in her mouth.

Veronica looked at her with an unreadable expression. As soon as their eyes met, Veronica looked away and Mack felt sick.

"I'm gonna puke," Mack groaned. Her legs felt like lead but she forced them to move. She quickly grabbed her backpack and rushed out of the cafeteria, leaving her tray behind. Mack kept her eyes focused on the exit doors and tried not to look at the stupids who were all laughing and pointing at her. Holding her backpack in front of her like a shield, she shouldered her way through the swinging double doors and into the hallway.

Some of the laughter died as the doors closed behind her, and she breathed a small sigh of relief. But she kept walking quickly, her sneakers slapping against the cheap tiles that lined the halls. Her heart felt like it was vibrating in her chest, palms slippery with sweat. Is this what a heart attack felt like? Maybe she was finally having a heart attack.

"Hey, wait!" Lila jogged beside her. "What are you doing?" Lila looped her arm through Mack's when she caught up with her.

"Running away from my problems," Mack said, eyes still straight ahead as she headed toward the parking lot.

"Don't you think actual running is required for that?"

"You know running in the halls is against school policy."

"Okay, well, stop power walking," Lila said, grasping Mack's sleeve and slowing her to a stop. "You're giving me flashbacks of when my mom joined that Oprah exercise club."

Mack faced her. She was breathing heavily and she was sure she looked crazy. "I have to get out of here. My life is over."

"First off, calm down the dramatics," Lila said with an amused smile. "And secondly, your life is not over."

"I'm not being dramatic!" Mack said, arms flailing at her sides and backpack falling to the ground. "Everyone knows I'm gay, Lila!"

Lila crossed her arms. "Are you worried about them knowing you're gay? Or knowing you're in love with Queen Bitch?"

"I'm not *in love* with her."

"Tomato, tomahto. No one will give a rat's ass about this tomorrow when someone else is pregnant. Then it'll be old news that you're a box bumper."

"A what?"

"A box—" Lila stopped herself and rolled her eyes. "You need to watch something other than Ellen every once in a while."

Mack rolled her eyes. "Just because you're *crude*."

"I'm not." Lila clapped her on the shoulder and steered her back toward the school parking lot. "Hey, look at the bright side. Maybe you can get a girlfriend now."

Mack groaned and bent down to pick up her backpack. "I guarantee you that's never going to happen."

Lila gave Mack a sympathetic look and squeezed her in a side hug. "So, ditch and go to the mall?"

It was tempting. The last thing Mack wanted to do was face any classmates for the rest of the day. Or ever. But the guilt of skipping gnawed at her stomach, almost as fiercely as the sickness and embarrassment from Chad finding her letter.

"No," she mumbled, "but can we go after? I really want a pretzel."

"Of course," Lila cooed at her, resting their heads together. "A cinnamon sugar one?"

Mack nodded. She felt a little better in her friend's embrace, not to mention the promise of a pretzel later.

"I just have to avoid everyone the rest of the day. How hard can that be?"

It was harder than Mack imagined. In every class, people stared and whispered as she passed. In the halls, people gave her a wide berth like she had some sort of disease. Luckily she only had one class with Veronica, so she just got there right before the bell and slipped into the seat in the very back. Then she made sure she was packed and ready to go as soon as the dismissal bell rang.

After school, Lila went to the mall with Mack as promised. They sat in the mall cafeteria with their cinnamon sugar pretzels. They were behind a large plant at Mack's request since the last thing she wanted to do was run into a classmate somewhere.

"Hey," Lila said, finally breaking the silence. "What about Jackie from third period? She's cute. And smells like a golf course."

Mack snorted in laughter. "First of all, that doesn't mean she's gay. Secondly, no."

Lila squinted. "Pretty sure that means she's gay."

"It could just mean she likes golf."

"And what's gayer than that?"

Mack rolled her eyes and leaned back in her chair. "She's not my type."

"What is your type? Veronica? I just don't get it."

"Maybe it's because you're straight. You just don't see it."

"I wouldn't say I'm *straight*," Lila said with a frown. "I think I could make out with a girl."

"But have you?"

"No."

"Then you're straight."

"Have you?" Lila said with a knowing eyebrow raise.

"No."

"Then you're straight?" Lila asked, popping a piece of pretzel into her mouth with a grin.

"No!" Mack pushed Lila's chair with her foot.

Something caught Lila's eye and she pointed her chin toward the other side of the mall. "Speak of the devil," Lila said.

Mack followed her gaze and saw Chad with his arm around Veronica. They were surrounded by a gaggle of other jocks and cheerleaders. Unfortunately Suzan, Veronica's bitchy best friend and right hand woman, was with her. Mack was sure she'd never seen Veronica without Suzan's blond hair and overly plucked eyebrows following obediently behind. She always looked like she'd smelled something nasty and her pointy features reminded Mack of a Doberman Pinscher or something else equally as terrifying. It was no secret that Suzan had always been jealous of Veronica. Mack wondered why Veronica even kept her around.

Just the sight of them made her stomach clench and her mouth go dry. She looked down at her pretzel, suddenly wanting to throw it away. "Maybe we should go. I feel too sick to eat my pretzel."

"They're blocking our exit." Lila pointed at the group of jocks close to them but still blocked by the plant. Mack groaned and stuffed another piece of the pretzel in her mouth. "I thought you were too sick to eat."

"Now I'm just stress eating."

They watched them through the plant branches. Mack stared at Veronica as she talked and laughed, her head tipped back. Mack sighed.

"Ugh, gross," Lila said with an eyeroll. "Let's get you focused on the girls you can actually get."

Mack sighed wistfully. "Like who?"

"There's a girl who works at the ear piercing place who's for sure gay," Lila said, finishing her pretzel.

"I think I'm just going to be single forever."

"Dramatic. You're a total catch. Get over it."

Mack felt herself flush and she tucked her hair behind her ear. "Sure," she said sarcastically.

"I would totally date you if we didn't…you know."

"If we didn't…what?" Mack tipped back in her chair. Lila stared back at her for a moment and Mack felt the legs of her chair tip just a little too far back. Her stomach dropped like a stone as she made one last desperate grab for the table. She grunted as her back hit the floor, pain shooting along her shoulders.

"Oh god, Veronica, is she stalking you?"

Mack opened her eyes and saw the entire jock table looking at her. To them it probably looked like she had just flopped out of the branches.

Meghan, the cheer co-captain, frowned at her. "She's totally stalking you."

Meghan was tall and beautiful with smooth flawless dark skin that was constantly on display. She would be right at home walking onto a fashion runway. That was most of the reason she seemed so frightening.

Mack scrambled to her feet while wiping cinnamon sugar off her cheeks. Lila looked back at her from behind the plant, looking just as horrified as Mack felt. The group stared at her like she had three heads—except for Beth, who was hiding her giggles behind a hand. Mack groaned and reached for Lila's wrist.

"We uh...we're just...bye!" Mack pulled Lila along behind her and out of the cafeteria. She heard snickers and scoffs as she passed the table of popular kids. Her cheeks burned so hot she was sure it was permanent.

"Could have been worse," Lila said with an awkward smile as they headed out of the mall.

"Just take me home," Mack groaned.

CHAPTER THREE

"My high school life is over." Mack sighed dramatically. She lay on her bed, pillow over her face while Lila sat on the opposite side and flipped through a magazine.

Looking up with a squint she asked, "Don't you have to have a life for it to be over?"

Mack threw her pillow at Lila, who just laughed and held it on her lap. She stuck her tongue out at her and went back to the magazine. Looking at the picture on the cover, Mack frowned. "Retirement magazine?"

Lila shrugged. "I like to plan ahead." She looked up at Mack. "Hey, maybe your parents will let you transfer."

Mack sat up on the bed, eyes wide. She forgot about her parents. Her stomach twisted and she reached blindly for Lila's hand, holding it in a vice grip.

"My parents."

"What about them?" Lila asked. She grimaced but Mack barely registered it.

"I haven't told them about the whole…gay thing. Fucking shit shit Christ!"

Lila pulled her hand away and leaned forward, holding Mack's face in both of her hands. She squished Mack's cheeks together so that she had fish lips. "You're having a meltdown. Your parents aren't going to find out."

Mack pushed Lila away, hands sliding from her cheeks as she did. "They're in the PTA, Lila. The only people nosier than cheerleaders and football players are their parents, trying to relive the glory of high school through their children. They're *for sure* gonna find out."

"You're such a drama queen," Lila said. "Mike and Carol will be cool with it."

With a groan, Mack pushed her friend's leg with her foot. "Don't call them by their first names. It creeps me out."

"What am I supposed to call them? Mr. and Mrs. Gomez?"

"Yes."

"As if."

Mack was too busy staring at the ceiling and pondering her fate to respond to Lila. Her parents were considered cool and were seemingly pretty liberal. But she had read the horror stories on the internet and after everything from preschool… They seemed cool with being gay in general, but everything was different when it was *your* child. She couldn't help but wonder what would happen if her parents were fine with gay people until she was one of them.

"I have to tell them," she sighed. "Better I tell them than they hear from someone else."

"You're not necessarily hiding it," Lila said, gesturing around the room at the walls. There were posters and magazine pages adorning the walls, mostly of female celebrities with a few dog pictures thrown in.

Mack shot Lila a look. "Shut up. I'm going down now."

"I'll go with you. For support."

Mack couldn't help but smile gratefully. "My emotional bra?"

"Obviously." Lila cupped her hands in front of her and made the motions as she said, "I support as well as lift and separate. Like a good bra should."

Mack laughed and shoved Lila's shoulder playfully. "All right. Better than walking in alone."

The knot in Mack's stomach tightened with each step down the stairs. It felt like she was walking to her own funeral. Maybe she could live with Lila after her parents kicked her out.

They were standing at the kitchen island making dinner together, the television playing softly in the background. Her mother looked up from chopping onions. "Hello, Mackenzie. If you two are looking for cookies, I'm afraid you guys cleaned us out last night."

Sickness suddenly flooded Mack's stomach and her hands shook. What was she doing?

"Oh, um…no cookies. Darn. Okay. Bye!" She turned on her heels to go back up the stairs, but Lila's arm across her stomach stopped her. Lila's dark eyes looked at her meaningfully.

"What are you doing? Just get it over with."

"I'm freaking out here," Mack whispered back, "I'll do it later."

"You'd rather one of their PTA friends tells them?" Lila asked.

"No."

"Then go." Lila grabbed Mack's shoulders and spun her around to face her parents again. They were both looking back at them with quizzical looks.

Mack forced a smile before taking a deep breath. "I um… have something to tell you."

They looked at each other and back at Mack. Her father finally spoke up. "Mackerel, is everything okay? Are you pregnant?"

"Oh god," Mack said putting a hand on her forehead, her cheeks heating again.

Carol shook her head and put her hand on her husband's arm. "Oh, honey, no. Mackenzie's a lesbian, remember?"

"Oh, right!"

Mack's jaw dropped at the words and she looked back at Lila who looked just as surprised as she was. She blinked at her parents who returned to cooking dinner.

"Um, I'm sorry," Mack said walking up to the kitchen island, her voice at least two octaves higher. "You knew?"

Mike and Carol looked at each other before looking back at their daughter. Mike shifted uncomfortably, setting down the bowl where he had been mashing potatoes.

"Well, we were worried you were into drugs—"

"What?" Mack squeaked.

"Yes! You spend so much time in your room just watching weird movies and well…I'm not proud of this, but I snooped on your computer." He shook his head shamefully.

Carol nodded. "Honey, no straight girl searches Kristen Stewart and animal rescues that much."

The tight muscles in Mack's chest wouldn't loosen and she felt like she might suffocate. "And you're…okay with it?"

"Of course!" Mike said, "Who do you take us for? The Cheneys? Sorry, are you too young to get that reference?"

"Dad, I think everyone knows how awful they were—"

"The Pences? Does that track better?"

"Sure."

"There, then who do you think we are? The Pences? As long as you're happy."

"And drug free," Carol added.

"And drug free," Mike agreed.

Mack stared at her parents for a moment before her whole body relaxed, a long breath escaping her lungs. She slumped onto a chair at the kitchen island, cradling her head in her hands and resting her elbows on the counter.

"Well that's one less thing to worry about," she murmured.

Lila sat on the stool next to her and rubbed Mack's shoulder. She was absolutely relieved and thrilled, but she felt like she didn't even have a minute to enjoy it. Her parents were fine with it; she didn't have to move out. But she still had to deal with all the kids at school.

"What's wrong?" Mike asked. He pushed his glasses onto the top of his bald head and looked at Mack.

"Nothing."

"Well," Lila said loudly over Mack, "one of the football players outed Mack and now she thinks her life is over."

"Kids these days. No manners."

"Want us to talk to their parents, Mackerel?" Mike asked.

"No! No. It'll just make everything worse and I'm enough of a leper as it is. I'll just handle it myself."

"So you're telling me that people are mean to you just because you like girls?" Mike shook his head.

"Are you so shocked by this?" Mack asked with a shrug. "You sent me to Catholic school."

"Yes, well. In our defense it's the best school in the area."

"Well, now I'm just going to have to deal with being tortured by football players for the rest of the year," Mack said, letting her head fall on the counter with a loud thump. Lila leaned over the counter and grabbed one of the carrots Carol was chopping.

"You know what you should do," Lila said, pointing at Mack with the half-eaten carrot. "You should steal all their stupid cheerleader girlfriends."

Mack barked out a laugh, "Yeah. Okay."

Carol brought out her 'encouraging mom' voice. "That's a great idea, Lila."

Lila gave Mack a triumphant grin, wiggling her eyebrows. "See? Great idea."

"Sure. I'll just walk into school tomorrow and steal one of the hottest girls in school."

"What's with the sarcasm, Mackerel?" Mike asked. "I think you can do it!"

"Yes, well you also told me I could be an astronaut when I was ten," Mack said, sliding off the counter stool.

"You could have."

"I'm horrible at math."

"That's not all that matters."

"It's literally impossible. Not only are they way out of my league, but they're all straight," Mack said gesturing for Lila to follow her. "We'll be upstairs. Enjoying my last night of being alive."

"Okay, well dinner will be ready in an hour. Lila, you staying?" Carol asked.

"Yes, please!" Lila said skipping toward the stairs, Mack close behind.

"You know," Mike called, "statistically, at least one of the cheerleaders has to swing both ways!"

"Thanks, Dad!" Mack groaned, taking the stairs two steps at a time back to her room.

CHAPTER FOUR

"Look at the bright side," Lila said as she pulled into the school parking lot. A couple of other students looked at the car as it drove up and Mack sank into her seat. "It can't get worse."

"Can't get worse. Yeah, right. That sounds more like a challenge."

"Everyone has probably forgotten about it already. It's old news," Lila said as she pulled into a parking spot.

Mack sat up in her seat again and looked around the parking lot. There were a few football players near the door but that was it. She sighed and undid her seat belt.

"Can't you drop me off around back or something?"

"You're being dramatic again." Lila checked her makeup in the visor mirror. She flipped it back up and looked at Mack. "It'll be fine."

Mack sighed, letting her forehead fall against the cold glass of the car window. "I should have stayed home."

"Drama queen. They've probably all forgotten by now," Lila said again as she got out of the car. "Come on, we're going to be late."

Sighing once more, Mack opened the door and practically slithered out. She could feel Lila's amused stare on her back. Slowly Mack walked toward the school. Lila bumped their hips together, knocking Mack off balance. She looped her arm in Mack's and gave her a reassuring squeeze.

"It'll be fine," she repeated more seriously. "I promise. I'll beat up anyone I need to. Okay?"

"You're too short to beat anyone up," Mack said with a reluctant smile. She tensed as they got nearer to the entrance where some football players still lurked.

"I can still beat anyone up."

Mack kept her eyes straight ahead as they got closer to the football players. She could feel her stomach clench and the prickling of sweat begin along her hairline. As they got past them, Mack squeezed Lila's arm. Mack let out a breath she didn't realize she was holding when the football players were finally behind them.

"See?" Lila patted Mack's hand that was still squeezing her arm. "Totally forgot."

"You're right," Mack mumbled. Lila bumped into her again as they got closer to their lockers.

"I usually am."

Suddenly a voice came over the speaker system. "Good morning, St. Patrick High. There is an assembly in the gym before classes. Please proceed to the gym now. Thank you."

Mack groaned and shut her locker. "Another one?"

"I wonder what it is this time," Lila mused. "Maybe they found another used condom behind the bleachers."

Mack shivered in disgust, shutting her locker a little harder than necessary. "Let's get this over with."

They followed the crowd to the gym and found seats in the back-row corner where they usually sat. The fewer people around, the better—also the furthest away from the prying eyes of the teachers looking for troublemakers, the better. Not that Mack or Lila ever had problems with that. The most trouble they ever caused was making each other giggle with a look or stupid joke.

All the students were settled just as Father Jorge approached the podium. A distinguished gentleman in his dark suit and stark white priest collar, Father Jorge was tall, lanky and had dark hair with streaks of grey that ran from his head down into his beard. His eyes were striking in the way a villain's in a kid's film were—harmless, yet somehow completely terrifying.

"Good morning, students," he said with a stiff smile.

"Morning," everyone echoed back at him.

"This morning I would like to talk to you about a disease that is sweeping our young people," he said in his booming voice.

Lila leaned over and whispered to Mack, "What do you think it is today? Drugs?"

Mack nodded. "Or if we're lucky it's premarital sex."

"Fingers crossed."

Beth, who was sitting in front of them, turned around and fixed Lila with a look. "We should be respectful."

Lila scoffed. "Of who? Father Jorge?"

"Yes. He had to nail his hands to a cross to be a priest," Beth said seriously. Her hazel eyes flickered to Mack and she smiled widely. "Hi, Mack."

"Hey," Mack said slowly, drawing in a deep breath and blushing under Beth's look. Beth waved once before turning around again and Mack exhaled noisily. Lila eyed her suspiciously and Mack could only shrug.

Father Jorge looked up solemnly. "The television and motion picture industries are telling us these things are okay. They're trying to corrupt our youth and tell us that it's okay to stray from the church's teachings. Instead of Mass, kids are going to Taco Bell and getting drunk off Baja Blasts."

Mack leaned over to Lila and whispered, "Do you think he even knows what Taco Bell is?"

"I've seen young minds corrupted by sex, violence, and drugs," Father Jorge continued. "But the one thing…that seems to be corrupting the youth of America more than anything…" He took a deep dramatic breath, "…is homosexuality."

Mack felt her stomach drop and her body instantly tense. Far too many faces turned to look at her, hiding in the back row. Beth turned to her and gave a sympathetic and slightly confused smile.

"Fuck me," Mack muttered, pulling the hood of her sweatshirt over her head as she sank down into her seat. She could feel the gazes of her peers on her and wished she could just disappear.

Father Jorge continued and Mack peeked out of her hood to see most of the students turn back around. "It is a disease that has taken ahold of our youth and corrupted the brightest minds. Something you must guard yourself against!"

"This is some bullshit is what it is," Lila mumbled under her breath.

Father Jorge paced the gym floor. "Do not let yourself be corrupted by the homosexual! They might offer you tempting things and feed you lies, but they are just trying to drag you into their sinful ways. Beware of their influence on you, lest they drag you down the path to hell."

He paused and slowly took in the entire room. Mack felt her stomach turn and clench, threatening to empty the contents of her stomach onto Beth sitting in front of her. She had heard all this before. It was nothing new. But that was before everyone knew she was a big ol' gay. Before it was easy to play innocent and play along with everything they were saying. Now it felt like everyone knew and there was no hiding.

"Students, let's stand and say a Hail Mary," Father Jorge finished.

Mack stood with the rest of the students and pulled her hood from her head to avoid being yelled at by a teacher. Lila reached for Mack's hand and squeezed as everyone began at once.

"Hail Mary full of grace. The Lord is with thee. Blessed are thou amongst women…"

Mack knew all the least populated hallways of the school. She knew just when to leave class to avoid the biggest crowds and how to get to her locker without being noticed. It was something she had perfected her freshman year, and now she used it to avoid the people staring at her after the assembly.

For almost all four years of high school she had successfully avoided being outed in any way. Most of that success was due to the fact that no one cared enough about her to bully her, let alone dig into her sexual preferences. She had enjoyed her time as an invisible teenager and had hoped that the rest of high school would continue that way. Now she was some kind of oddity, something to be gawked at.

She turned the corner and saw her locker. Most students were already in their classrooms so she quickly walked down the hall. She was almost there when someone stepped into her path. Mack stumbled as she stopped a little too quickly and blinked at the girl in front of her. She was chewing a piece of gum that looked too big for her mouth and Mack found it hard to stare at anything else.

"Hello?" Mack said looking at her nervously.

"The football team said you might be interested in joining the softball team," she said, clearly sizing Mack up. Her face flushed and she shoved her hands in the pocket of her sweatshirt. "You're a little small, though."

Mack frowned. "I'm not *that* small."

The girl reached out and squeezed Mack's arm as if testing it. Mack took a step back.

"Yeah, you're a little noodly, but I'll take it." She shoved a flier at Mack and walked away without preamble.

Mack grabbed for the flier before it fell to the ground and read it. *Join the Softball team today!*

She crushed it in her fist as she opened her locker, her stomach still in knots. She felt her eyes burning but refused to give in to it. It wasn't enough for the football team to out her, they had to get other people in on it too. She threw the flier into her locker and slammed it shut before turning back toward the classroom.

As soon as she stepped inside, all eyes turned on her and she gritted her teeth. She took her seat in the back and shrunk down into her chair. Lila, who had the seat in front of her, turned around quickly.

"You've been taking your secret pathways?"

"Yeah, but it didn't work," Mack whispered as the teacher stood up to start the lesson. "Someone told the softball team I wanted to join. Can you imagine? Me playing softball?"

Lila hesitated for a moment. "Maybe you'd meet a cute girl."

"If there were any cute queer girls in this school…er…queer girls in general…I would have found them by now."

Lila smirked. "Not picky then?"

"Shut up," Mack blushed, pushing Lila's shoulder so that she turned around.

Mack sat on the other side of Principal Berkley's desk, fiddling with the sleeve of her sweatshirt and waiting for him to say…something.

She had been called out of PE, which was great, but it also meant she was sitting in front of her principal in her PE uniform, which felt equally embarrassing and vulnerable. She didn't even pretend to wonder what it was about. She was *sure* at least one teacher had heard about the fiasco in the cafeteria.

"Well, Mackenzie," Principal Berkeley said, snapping a folder shut that she assumed was her own. "You have a stellar record."

"T-thank you?" Mack asked, frowning.

"Because of that, you'll just get a warning," he said with a small smile, folding his hands on his desk.

"A warning for...what?" Mack asked as her heart pounded wildly in her chest. Her brain was furiously trying to figure out if she should play stupid or just try and not die from embarrassment.

He fixed her with a look, a small condescending smile. "Mackenzie, we know what it's about. I heard you have been talking about certain...things. Same-sex relationships and such. You know that these are things we can't talk about here."

Mack just shrugged, trying to look disaffected. "Um...okay."

She felt like she was going to barf. The adrenaline coursing through her veins had two effects. First, she definitely felt like she was going to be sick all over Principal Berkley's desk. Secondly, she had a thousand practiced words on her tongue for all the times she had imagined this happening. All the scholarly articles and bits of scripture she had stored back in her mind for a moment like this rattled against the back of her teeth, but she just bit her tongue.

He just stared at her for what felt like ten whole minutes. "All right...as long as we're on the same page here—"

"Can I go now? It's the mile run in PE today and that's my favorite."

"You're free to go," Principal Berkeley said, leaning back in his chair to show that she was dismissed.

Mack was up and out of her chair before he even had a chance to call her back. As she walked out into the hall, she took a deep breath and tried to calm her shaking hands.

"Fuck. This."

* * *

Mack had gone home that night and replayed the moment with Principal Berkley in her head over and over again, each time with a new and exciting argument that would make him rethink the entire school policy. She told herself that she would use these arguments on her classmates, but deep down she knew better. So when the bullying and quips started, Mack wasn't surprised that she just let it.

One day everyone kept giving her plaid shirts, the next day it was cat adoption papers. But the final straw came on Thursday after school. Mack went to her locker, practically bracing herself for some sort of weird attack. She undid the lock and opened the door. Like she guessed would happen, a wave of small pink papers fluttered out. Her entire locker had been stuffed with coupons of some sort. Mack breathed deeply through her nose just as Lila joined her.

Each little dig, each little "joke" made a flame of anger grow in Mack. She'd always considered herself an even-tempered person, but she also hadn't had a reason to truly get angry until this point. Her previous track record of sailing through high school invisible and unscathed seemed to be over, and that was enough for her to be ticked off about.

"Shit," Lila said, picking up a coupon and reading it out loud. "Two for one at Pink Taco. Go ahead, eat the place out."

Lila cackled and grabbed a few more of the coupons. Mack looked at her incredulously and shut her locker again.

"It's not funny." Mack said, knocking the coupon from Lila's hand so that it fluttered to the floor. She sobered immediately, nodding solemnly.

"You're right." She grabbed another coupon off the floor to look. "But you have to admit that saying is pretty golden."

"I'm fucking tired of this," Mack said, ignoring her. "I'm tired of the looks and the fucking…" She picked some coupons off the ground and shoved them in Lila's face. "This!"

Lila put her hand on Mack's shoulder and squeezed. "I hate to say this, but it could be a lot worse."

"Excuse me? I know it could be worse. But that doesn't mean this doesn't fucking suck too!"

Lila threw her arms up in frustration. "Then what are you going to do? You're the most passive person I know!"

Mack stood a little straighter. "I am not."

"You're my best friend, and I love you more than anything. But you are."

The small fire that was burning in Mack's chest suddenly exploded. She adjusted her backpack on her shoulder and turned on her heels. The worn rubber of her tennis shoes slapped against the tile of the hallway as she started out of the building.

"Mack!" Lila called out to her, following behind.

The football field was separated from the school by another parking lot where all the cool kids usually sat. The parking lot gave way to grass where the bleachers looked out over the field. Mack walked past the bleachers to see the football team practicing on the field.

"Mack! What are you doing?" Lila called behind her.

Her focus was on Chad, who was standing on the edge of the field waiting for a pass. He didn't notice as she stalked up to him, her heart racing. Out of her peripheral vision, she saw a football hurtling toward them and casually hit it to the ground right as he was about to catch it. Chad blinked for a moment before looking over at Mack.

"What the fu—?"

"What the hell is your problem?"

Chad stared at her for a moment, something coming over his face. "Huh?"

"Don't play stupid with me," Mack said pointing a finger at him that felt more threatening than she was sure it looked, especially with Chad having at least a foot on her in height. "I know it's you who's been orchestrating all that shit."

Chad scoffed as Lila came up next to Mack. "I don't know what you're talking about."

Lila threw one of the coupons at him and Mack was pleased to see he had the decency to blush at the very least. He shrugged and crossed his arms. "So what?"

"So just *leave me alone*," Mack said firmly in a voice she didn't recognize. "I didn't do anything to you! You can't just go around outing people."

Chad chuckled. "You didn't do anything to me, huh? You were scamming on my girl!"

"I wasn't *scamming* on anyone," Mack said. "I barely ever *talked* to Veronica."

"You have a crush on her."

"So does half the school! That's no fucking excuse! I wrote a *note*. You outed me to every Neanderthal here!"

Chad looked confused for a moment, then started laughing. "Maybe if you weren't such a freak, this wouldn't have happened! Did you really think you had a chance with her anyway?" He paused for effect as his buddies gathered around them.

Mack felt her chest tightening so painfully with anxiety she thought she might pop a rib. Tears of anger burned behind her eyes and she willed them to stay in place.

"She's a cheerleader," Chad said with a smirk. "Why don't you try someone your own speed? Like the lunch lady?"

The other football players started laughing and something inside of Mack snapped. She strode up to Chad so she could poke him hard in the chest. To her surprise and delight, he stumbled back a little in shock.

"Fuck you!" she shouted. "I could get a cheerleader if I wanted!"

The football players laughed louder and Mack felt her ears tint red.

"Yeah, right," Chad said, shaking his head.

"I can and I will!"

"Um," Lila said quietly behind her, "Mack."

The football players just laughed louder and it spurred Mack on.

"Fuck you!" she said pointing at Chad. She pointed at the rest of the football players. "Fuck *all* of you! I'm not going to just get one cheerleader. I'm going to steal all your girlfriends!"

The football team laughed even louder, the sound almost deafening. She felt Lila tugging on the back of her sweatshirt but ignored it.

"I'd like to see you try!" Chad said.

"Good! Because that's exactly what I'm going to do!" Mack spun around as the football players practically howled in laughter. With one last surge of confidence, she turned back around to yell. "And the lunch lady is very nice! I'm sure once you take the hairnet off she's very attractive!"

With one more satisfied nod of her head, she stomped off the field, passing a very shocked looking Lila. Their shoulders brushed and it knocked her out of her daze.

"Um, Mack..."

"What?" Mack asked, hands clenched in fists at her sides as she walked toward the bleachers. She could hear blood rushing through her ears, heart practically vibrating.

"I told you to get one cheerleader. One!" Lila said, jogging to catch up with her. "Not *all* of them!"

Some of Mack's anger subsided and panic took over. She let out a long breath through her nose as she ducked under the bleachers. As soon as they were out of sight of the football players, she whispered, "Holy shit! I just made the worst mistake of my life."

Lila grimaced. "Don't be dramatic. There was that time you tried to eat a tablespoon of cinnamon."

"This is your fault! You and my stupid parents. You all convinced me I could get a cheerleader—"

"Yes, *one* cheerleader—"

"You all planted this seed. I would have never even thought of anything like that if you hadn't planted the idea. It wormed its way into my subconscious and came spewing out at the most inconvenient time!"

Mack felt her lungs struggling to expand as she gave into her panic. Her chest started to burn as she hyperventilated, flailing her hands in front of her helplessly. Lila stood in front of her and held her arms down at her sides, giving her a serious look.

"Calm down, Spazz McGee." Lila shook her a little. "It's okay. Breathe in."

She took a deep breath in and Mack struggled, but mimicked her.

"Good. Now breathe out."

Mack breathed out with Lila. They did it a few more times until Mack breathed normally and her lungs stopped burning.

"Better?" Lila asked with a warm smile. Mack nodded and couldn't help but smile back. "Good," Lila said. "You can do this."

Mack felt some of the panic leak back into her chest and Lila shook her lightly.

"Hey, hey," Lila said trying to get Mack's attention. "Don't freak out. Just listen to me."

Mack nodded, unconvinced.

"You got this. Okay?" Lila said a little slower. "You're a sexy, confident woman."

Mack pulled a face and Lila shook her harder. "No, you have to believe it. Olivia Wilde has nothing on you. Say it."

Mack frowned and shifted uncomfortably. "I'm…" She struggled but finally got the word out. "S-sexy?"

"Yes!" Lila bounced on the balls of her feet. "You're sexy! Say it again!"

Mack couldn't help but feel a little of the confidence leak into her. "I'm sexy!"

"There you go!" Lila beamed, before she screamed, "You're so fucking sexy!"

"I'm so sexy!"

Lila started bouncing in excitement and Mack couldn't help but bounce with her. "Yeah! Now go get all those cheerleader bitches!"

Mack flinched a little, but Lila's energy was contagious. "I'll get all those cheerleader…bitches!"

Lila screamed in Mack's face and Lila screamed back. Mack started to jog back toward the school and Lila smacked her ass as she went. Mack continued jogging but couldn't help but feel her confidence drain.

"Shit," she said under her breath.

CHAPTER FIVE

"Come out of there!" Lila called from the other side of the dressing room door. "Let me see what you got on!"

Mack frowned at herself in the floor length mirror, the unflattering fluorescent lights flickering overhead. She smoothed out the purple dress she had on and sighed, opening the door for Lila. She came bursting in, locking the door behind her before looking Mack over.

"Oh, damn, who knew you had those legs on you?" Lila lifted the edge of Mack's skirt a bit to get a better look. "You shave?" Mack pushed her hands away and looked back in the mirror.

"What are you talking about? It's not like I never wear a bathing suit or shorts around you," she said turning to look at her dress from the back. "I don't know if I like it."

Lila's eyes roamed Mack's body slowly and for some reason it made Mack squirm, but not uncomfortably.

"You look...really pretty," Lila said softly. Her eyes lingered on Mack's neck for a moment before darting back up to her eyes. "Why don't you like it?"

"I don't feel comfortable," Mack said, blushing under Lila's looks. "I don't really like dresses."

"Let me get you some pants and some cute button-ups or something. Go with the tomboy look."

"That's not too...masculine?" Mack asked, embarrassed.

Lila shook her head. "Who gives a fuck? You're gonna look fine as hell. Wear whatever makes you comfortable. Plus, anything will be an improvement from your old jeans and sweatshirts."

Mack looked back in the mirror. "Fine. Help me undress."

She turned so that Lila could reach her zipper. She pulled it down slowly, fingers following the zipper down Mack's spine. Mack suppressed a shiver and looked into the mirror. Her eyes met Lila's who was just as flushed.

"I'll get you some good stuff," Lila said before leaving the dressing room.

"That's...weird," Mack said, rolling her shoulders and trying to shake off the fluttery feeling in her stomach. "Super weird."

Mack stood in front of her bed, completely at a loss. Bags filled with new clothes spilled out. She was still reeling from the day before when she'd told all the football players she was going to steal their girlfriends. If only she had a time machine she could use. She would go back and slap herself across her stupid mouth before she could make a statement that bold.

But time travel didn't exist and Mack was stuck in the present with her impulse control issues to keep her company, not to mention the memory of her failure that would haunt her forever.

Lila was lying on her stomach on Mack's bed on the other side of the bags, feet kicked up in the air as she flipped through one of Mack's old magazines. She seemed oblivious to Mack's crisis.

Mack felt sick to her stomach.

"What if I just...dropped out?" She pulled out a shirt from her closet and wrinkled her nose at it before letting it drop to the floor. Discarded clothes littered the floor around her feet— things to give to charity to make room for her new clothes.

"You can't do that." Lila sighed, not even sparing Mack a glance.

Mack grunted and shoved all her clothes to one side so that she could look into the deep depths of the closet. "I know. I have to steal the cheerleaders or I'll look like a coward, and when I try to steal them and inevitably fail, then I will *still* look like an idiot."

"You're stuck in a real Catch-22," Lila said disinterestedly.

Mack frowned and turned to look at Lila. "Is that how you use that?"

Lila looked up at her and shrugged. "Pretty sure."

Mack turned back to her bed. From deep in one bag, she pulled out a blue button-up shirt Lila insisted was her color. She held it up and quickly put it on. Rolling up the sleeves a little, she turned back to Lila. "What do you think?"

Lila looked up from the magazine and blinked. The magazine page fell from her fingers and fluttered back to the bed. "I...it looks...You look good."

"Yeah?" Mack said, stomach warming a little. Lila nodded and Mack's stomach flipped as her best friend's gaze scanned her body. She licked her lips. "Um...Lila?"

Lila blinked and looked at Mack, her own cheeks tinted. She cleared her throat before looking back down at her magazine.

"Who would have known a clean shirt would make that much of a difference, huh?"

Mack smoothed down the front. She pulled a brush from her dresser drawer. Considering herself in the mirror, she brushed her hair to one side before shaking her head and parting it the other direction.

"Wow and you're brushing your hair too."

"I need to do what I can to impress girls, Lila," Mack said, finally settling on a hairstyle. Lila stood up and walked behind Mack, who was still messing with her shirt in the mirror. Mack caught Lila's gaze and smiled at her. Lila wrapped her arms around Mack's waist from behind and Mack leaned back into her, her hands covering Lila's.

"Just be your wonderful self," Lila said lightly, resting her chin on Mack's shoulder. Mack felt affection settle in her chest as Lila smirked and quickly added, "It'll trick them into thinking you're awesome."

Mack rolled her eyes and squeezed Lila's hands with her own. "Asshole."

"And that's why we're friends." She squeezed Mack around the waist once and dropped her arms. "Now let's go before we're late."

"Fine," Mack said, grabbing her backpack and some boots she never wore in favor of her usual sneakers. They were a pair of simple black boots she had begged her mom to get her after seeing Kristen Stewart wear some similar ones in a magazine. "Let's go…attempt to talk to girls."

"That's the spirit," Lila said, clapping her friend on the shoulder.

"You ready?" Lila asked Mack as they stood in front of the doors to the school.

Mack nodded curtly, tugging at the hem of her shirt one more time. She pushed her sunglasses up her nose, held her chin high and pushed open the doors. If her life was one of those cheesy high school movies, she'd be walking in slow motion while a mysterious wind blew her hair back perfectly. But it wasn't. The combined glare of the fluorescent lights in the hall with her mirrored sunglasses made it hard to see, but she kept them on. It made her feel cooler. More confident. Plus they hid the raw animal terror she felt when she saw other people looking at her like she was a brand new person.

Mack got to her locker and felt eyes on her. She looked around and spotted Beth standing a couple of yards away at her own locker staring at her. Beth smiled shyly and Mack smiled back with a small nod. Beth's smile got wider and she offered a small wave in Mack's direction just as someone stepped into their line of sight.

Mack looked up to see Veronica standing in front of her, arms crossed and an eyebrow raised. She couldn't help the way her stomach flipped. She was just so beautiful. It was like looking into the eyes of an angel dressed in a cheerleading uniform.

"Your plan isn't going to work," Veronica said firmly. It was only then that Mack even noticed Suzan next to her.

Mack blinked, regaining her ability to speak as she looked between the two cheerleaders. She felt Lila standing behind her, probably trying to look intimidating.

"My plan?"

Lila kicked the back of her foot and it jogged Mack's memory. Right. Stealing cheerleaders. She felt herself blush just as a girl Mack had honestly never seen before passed them— while smiling shyly at her. Mack smirked and looked back at Veronica, some of her confidence restored.

"I wouldn't be too sure about that," she said smugly, pushing her sunglasses on the top of her head.

"Listen, just because you wore a shirt that actually fits you for once and decided to brush your teeth, doesn't mean you can get any of my girls," Veronica said with her own smirk.

Mack chuckled as she opened her locker. "Wow, that was probably one of the gayest things I've ever heard."

Veronica rolled her eyes and looked at Mack with a serious scowl. Mack hated that she still found it incredibly hot.

"I'm not going to let you ruin my plans. Do you understand?" Veronica said dangerously. "We're going to win Nationals. We *need* to win Nationals. And I'm going to lead the team to victory and the Ex-Priests for Student Athletes Coalition isn't going to support a team full of lesbians."

"Because a bunch of perverted old men are the judges?"

"No, idiot. They're our sponsor," Suzan piped up. Veronica shot her a look and she shrank back again.

Mack said sarcastically, "Well I know it would suck for you to not have another trophy in the case gathering dust—"

"It's more than that," Veronica interrupted. Her tough demeanor softened for a moment and Mack felt like reaching out and putting a hand on her arm. Thankfully she didn't act on that impulse because Suzan probably would have bitten her hand off. "I need a win this year to help me get into college. You'd be ruining my future."

"I highly doubt Mack dating some of the girls on your team would jeopardize your chances of becoming a professional cheerleader and marrying rich," Lila deadpanned. Veronica flinched as something crossed her face that looked an awful lot like vulnerability before it was gone and her scary face was back.

"Whatever," she said turning back toward Mack. "All of my cheerleaders are members of the High on Jesus Club *and* the Celibacy Club. There's no way you're going to get your filthy little paws on them."

Just then a cheerleader passed them, her belly protruding and pretty obviously pregnant. Mack raised her eyebrow and looked back at Veronica who couldn't hide her blush.

"Yeah, we see how well that's going," Mack said, getting her books out of her locker and closing it. She turned on her heels and called over her shoulder. "See you later, Ronnie."

"What an idiot," Lila said as they headed toward their shared English class.

Mack bumped against Lila briefly. "She's not an idiot. She's super smart. Straight A's and everything."

Lila pretended to gag as they walked into the classroom. "She's a tool. You just can't see it because you're in love with her."

Mack tried to hide her smile. "Not *in love*…I just see the parts of her no one else does."

"Like her tits?" Lila smirked as they got into their respective seats. "Because I'm pretty sure everyone can see those."

Mack felt like her face was burning when she shot Lila a look. She pulled out her English textbook just as the sound of everyone's phones buzzing at the same time went through the classroom. Everyone pulled out their phones. Mack just looked around confused. Some people looked back at her and others ducked their heads together as they whispered.

"Oh, shit," Lila said. Mack looked over at her as Lila looked at her phone. Lila sighed. "Your precious Veronica just tweeted to everyone that they should call animal control if they've had contact with you."

Mack reached for Lila's phone and snatched it from her hand. "I didn't know you got Ronnie's twits. I didn't even know you had a tweeter."

Lila grinned like she'd just heard the funniest joke. "I bet you'd like Veronica's twits all up in your tweeter."

"I told you I don't like technology!" Mack hissed, tossing Lila her phone and feeling like she'd missed a joke somewhere.

Lila slipped her phone back in her pocket just as the teacher, Ms. Inkelbam, stood up to start class. Lila leaned closer to Mack from the seat beside her.

"Aren't you a little upset that Veronica is saying this shit about you to the cheerleaders you're trying to bag?"

Mack shrugged. Her confidence and bravado were completely based on the fact that she didn't quite believe she was actually going to have to follow through with her threat.

"Just means I'll have to turn on twice the charm," Mack said, winking at Lila. She flipped her pencil in the air in a way that should have looked cool. And it would have if it hadn't hit her in the eye. Mack slapped her hand over her eye as it started watering in pain. "Ow! Shit. Fuck. Balls!"

Lila snorted and Mack flipped her off with the hand that wasn't covering her injured eye.

"Mack!" Ms. Inkelbam called from the front of the classroom. Mack sat up a little straighter and looked at her teacher. She was young with dark hair in a hipster cut and chunky glasses. She almost looked like someone you'd see working on their laptop at an artisan coffee shop while nursing one tea all day. Mack had taken a liking to her as queer girls usually do with their English teachers for whatever mythical reason. Admittedly she'd had a small crush on her their freshman year, but that quickly went away with how familiar Ms. Inklebam tried to act with the students. Still, Mack and Lila would always volunteer to help her take down her classroom at the end of the year or to decorate for whatever themed week she thought would make the lessons more fun. It bred a sort of familiarity between them that Mack was sure she'd talk about in therapy someday.

"Yes, Ms. Inklebam?" Mack said dropping her hand from her eye, which she hoped wasn't too red.

"Get up here with your bad self!"

Mack groaned and looked over at Lila, who shrugged. She slipped out of her desk and headed toward the front of the classroom. Mack smiled at her cautiously.

"Hey there Macky Mack. Mackster," the teacher said awkwardly.

Ms. Inklebam was always trying to use language that Mack assumed she thought was *en vogue*. She sounded like a character from an after-school teen drama but she said it with such earnest that Mack could never find it anything but endearing.

"What can I help you with?"

The teacher noticed Mack's injured eye. "What's going on here? Do you have pink eye or something?"

"Ew, no," Mack said rubbing at it with the back of her hand. "I poked it with a pencil."

"There's no shame in pink eye. People say it's a childhood disease but I got it from changing my cat's litter once."

Mack tried not to look as grossed out as she felt. "Um…"

"Anyways," Ms. Inkelbam continued, waving her hand in front of her face, "I need you to do me a favor. I need you to tutor Beth."

"What? Why?" Mack stuttered, shoving her hands in her pockets nervously, as she glanced over her shoulder at Beth. The cheerleader was staring down at the paper in front of her with a frown.

Ms. Inklebam leaned closer to Mack and whispered. "She needs a lot of help and so far no one has been able to get her anywhere near a passing grade. Beth is sweet but I don't grade on likability here."

Mack rubbed the back of her neck. "I mean…She's not *that* stupid, is she?"

"We don't use the word 'stupid'," Ms. Inklebam said very seriously, even with mirth dancing behind her eyes. "She just is in need of extra help."

"I don't know. I've never tutored anyone before," Mack said.

"Basically, I just need you to help her pass. Or cheat," the teacher said with a shrug. "Anything that will get her to pass. She must have help in all her other classes because for some reason this is the only one she's not passing."

"Isn't there someone else who can do it?" Mack asked hopefully. She wasn't a bad student, but she certainly wasn't a *good* one. She got decent grades but barely had the motivation to do her own homework, let alone help someone else with theirs.

Ms. Inkelbam sighed. "You're literally my last resort. Literally. I even asked the English as a second language kid before you. But…" Ms. Inklebam leaned even further forward and Mack worried she was going to fall out of her seat. "I heard about what happened in the cafeteria yesterday."

Mack felt her stomach drop and panic rise like bile in her throat. "What?"

"Yeah. The whole school knows. They've even started a fund to cleanse you. But that's not important. I don't care who you want to kiss. I just want to help you make *friends*."

Ms. Inkelbam winked at her and Mack just frowned in confusion. She sighed and lowered her voice even more.

"What I'm saying is, I want to help you," she said conspiratorially. "You're trying to get all the cheerleaders, and I'm giving you a reason to hang out with one. Alone."

Mack was still hung up on the cleansing fund. "How does everyone know about this?"

"We're high school teachers. We're in on all the gossip too," she said with a shrug. "Now just tell me before the end of class if you're going to tutor Beth. Okay?"

Mack just nodded and headed back to her desk. She was sure there was no color left in her face and that she was about to be sick.

"What was that about?" Lila whispered.

Mack blinked as she tried regain her composure. "She... wants me to tutor Beth."

"Seriously?"

"Did you know that the *entire* staff knows I'm gay? They have a cleansing fund for me and everything."

"Duh. The principal just had a talk with you. But wait." Lila shook her head and held her hand up for Mack to stop. "Hold up, go back. She wants you to tutor Beth? That's awesome."

"Did you miss the part about the cleansing fund?"

"Don't be dense, Mack," Lila said, practically falling out of her seat with excitement. "Beth is the gayest cheerleader. She's the perfect girl to start your plan with."

The possibilities suddenly clicked in Mack's mind and her eyes got wide. A tutoring session would basically be a study date with Beth. Just the thought made her throat close with anxiety. At least Beth was clueless. Maybe if Mack made a move on her and it didn't work out, she could play it off as...something else. Still, Mack shook her head.

"Did you smoke out before class again?" She frowned. "I told you, you're gonna get caught—"

"Get real. It's only Tuesday, and you're deflecting!"

Mack rolled her eyes and chanced another look at Beth. She was doodling something that looked like a unicorn in the corner of the page.

"She's not gay," Mack whispered out of the corner of her mouth.

"Mack, look at her nails. They're short. She has to be a little gay."

Mack saw Beth's blunt nails painted a sparkly pink. Beth's eyes met hers and Mack blushed. "You're wrong. A lot of girls wear their nails short."

"Cheerleaders?" Lila countered with a look that told Mack she thought she had won this argument. Though if she was being honest, Lila had a point, but it still didn't convince Mack that Beth was gay. There was no evidence pointing toward it. At all. Mack tried to remember if Beth had ever had a boyfriend. She couldn't recall one, even with all the other cheerleaders pairing off like it was Noah's Ark. Mack just figured it was because Beth didn't care, that she was too spacey to actually get herself a boyfriend.

But Mack also knew there was no way she was going to win this argument with Lila.

"Fine," Mack sighed. She adjusted the collar of her shirt and turned back toward Beth. She was still doodling and Mack cleared her throat to get the other girl's attention. Beth looked up at her, a slow smile crawling over her features. Mack felt her mouth go dry at the sight. Beth had always been nice to her, she was nice to everyone actually.

"Hey," Beth murmured, gazing at Mack.

"Hi…um," Mack shook her head for being so ridiculous. She was a gay mess. Just a smile from a girl and she was unable to speak? Ridiculous. "Ms. Inkelbam wants me to tutor you."

Beth frowned and pushed some of her long dark hair behind her ear. "But…I have an F. My mom says that stands for fantastic."

"There's…always room for improvement?" Mack offered, with a small smile of her own.

Beth still frowned but nodded. "I guess. My cat has a therapy appointment after school, but then I'm free."

"Your…" Mack shook her head. "Okay. I'll see you later tonight then. Six?"

"Sure," Beth said with one more smile before turning back to her paper. Mack noticed Ms. Inkelbam giving her a thumbs up from the front of the classroom. She awkwardly returned it and slumped down in her seat for the rest of class.

"Just brush your hair again, pick a new shirt, redo your deodorant and you're good to go," Lila said, already going through Mack's closet for new clothes. Mack began to unbutton her shirt as she went into the bathroom. She brushed her hair, put on fresh deodorant and had begun to brush her teeth when Lila threw a shirt at her. It landed haphazardly on her head before she snatched it up.

Mack slipped on her simple, black, low-cut shirt and walked back into the bedroom. She held out her arms for Lila's approval. Lila looked at her from her spot on the bed and nodded.

"You look hot," Lila said. "Just throw those same boots on from this morning and you're good to go."

Mack sighed and flopped on the bed next to Lila. Her stomach was churning and she was starting to regret the fast food they'd gotten on the way home.

"Maybe I should cancel," she muttered, throwing her arm over her eyes.

"Why? This is the perfect opportunity!"

"I mean what if…" Mack chewed the inside of her cheek. Lila pushed herself up on her elbow so she could look at Mack.

"Spill."

Mack groaned and shook her head. "What if we…I've never actually kissed a girl."

Lila pulled Mack's arm from her face. "I know. But you kissed Billy Eggers freshman year. It's the same thing, just… less gross."

"Kissing a girl is different than kissing a boy," Mack insisted, playing with the edge of her shirt.

"It's not that different."

Mack frowned. "Are you telling me you've kissed a girl?" Lila blushed and Mack gawked at her. "What the hell? You lied! You said you never had."

"It was nothing," Lila said, trying to wave it off. "I didn't want to make you jealous."

"When?"

"Remember two summers ago when I was at that weekend Jesus camp my mom wanted me to go to?"

"St. Catherine's Summer Camp?"

"Yes."

"You kissed a girl there?" Mack practically yelled. "And you didn't tell me? What about being best friends!"

"Like I said, it wasn't a big deal. It was barely a kiss, and… Honestly, she wasn't that cute. And I didn't want you to think I punched my gay card before you."

Mack felt her stomach turn for a different reason she couldn't quite pinpoint. She tried to ignore it.

"Are you…" Mack hesitated. It felt weird to be asking her best friend of—well, basically her whole life—such a weird question. "Are you gay?"

"I don't like labels," Lila said, her brow furrowed in thought. "I don't know. I've never thought about it."

Mack sat up. "I'm…if you want to talk about it."

"I don't. It's not a big deal."

"But if it becomes a big deal…I'm here," Mack said, reaching for Lila's hand. "I'm obviously not the best at the whole being out thing. But I definitely know I like girls."

Lila squeezed Mack's hand. "Thanks, bitch."

Mack rolled her eyes and hit Lila with a pillow. She squealed and jumped off the bed while Mack laughed.

"Come on," Lila said, eyes sparkling with mischief. "Let's go get you a cheerleader."

Mack stood in front of Beth's door with her backpack slung over her shoulder. She'd been staring at if for what felt like forever, though she was sure it had only been a couple of minutes. She inhaled deeply and knocked. The seconds ticked by like hours until Beth opened the door.

For a moment, Mack was blinded by the bright light streaming from behind Beth. Mack wondered if this was the first time she'd seen her out of her cheer uniform. She was wearing what looked like track shorts and a simple T-shirt with a neckline just deep enough to frame the gold cross necklace laying against her chest. And she held a big orange cat who stared at Mack with wide eyes.

"Um."

"Oh. You're here," Beth said looking behind Mack like she was expecting someone else. "I thought this was a joke the team was playing on me."

"Um...yep. I'm here," Mack said bouncing nervously on the balls of her feet.

Beth blinked at her for a moment. "So...This isn't a joke?"

"No?" Mack said slowly with a frown.

"Okay. Come in then." Beth closed the door behind them and Mack nervously removed her boots. The cat stared at her, tail moving restlessly in Beth's arms. Mack straightened up and Beth held the cat out toward her.

"This is Tobias," Beth said, squeezing him once before dropping him to the floor. He looked up at Mack for a moment before darting away. "He likes you."

"Oh, um...that's...nice," Mack said, adjusting her backpack on her shoulder. Beth started toward the stairs and Mack just watched for a moment before realizing she was supposed to follow. Pictures of Beth growing up adorned the staircase. In all of them she was smiling brightly at the camera in fluffy dresses until she graduated to the cheer uniform Mack was used to seeing her in.

Beth had always been a bit of an enigma. She always hung out with the cheerleaders as was expected, but it seemed like she was always a bit on the outside. The only comments Mack ever really heard about her was that she was dumb. Mack always thought it was mean and not completely fair. She was sure Chad was ten times dumber than Beth. In their brief interactions through the years, Mack mostly just thought Beth was funny. Even if she wasn't sure if Beth was *trying* to be funny half the time. She'd always been sweet and didn't make fun of people in the subtle ways the other cheerleaders sometimes would.

She got to Beth's door and saw a giant Taylor Swift poster tacked to it. Mack sighed. "For sure straight."

"What?" Beth called as she sat on the bed.

"Nothing." She looked around awkwardly before deciding to sit on the other side of the bed from Beth, her backpack between them. She looked around and was a bit overwhelmed by the amount of pink. An unbelievable number of Beanie Babies sat on what seemed like every surface. Mack sighed. The evening was going to be a bust before it even started. She couldn't help but feel a little relieved and gave Beth a genuine smile as she pulled her notebook out of her backpack. Now they could actually just study.

"So, what do you know about Emily Dickinson?" Mack asked, flipping to her notes.

"That her last name is dirty and she was a hermit," Beth replied with a twinge of pride in her voice. Mack stared at her for a moment, waiting for her to continue.

"Okay, um…What about her poetry?"

Beth pursed her lips in thought. "I know she was gay. Like you, which is why I wasn't allowed to do a paper on her."

"That's...ridiculous. Okay then let's start by going over her poem that we're studying this week."

She put her English book between them, open to the correct page, but Beth just continued to stare at her.

"So you are?"

"Am...what?" Mack said even as her stomach churned nervously.

Beth put her hands over Tobias's ears and Mack wondered for a second where the cat even came from. Then Beth whispered, "Gay."

Mack felt sick and she just cleared her throat. "Um...so Emily Dickinson—"

"You didn't answer my question."

"Yes!" Mack snapped. "Okay I am. Yes. Can we move on now?"

She braced herself for some sort of fallout. She wondered what it would be. Maybe Beth would say something rude or even kick her out. It could really be either one. Here Mack thought they'd be able to make it at least part of the way through the night until the whole being queer thing came up. She should have known better.

"You don't look like a sinner," Beth said with such a sincerely confused face that Mack felt her defenses crumbling.

"I...thank you? I guess."

"You know," Beth folded her hands in her lap. "I think you're really nice so I don't care what people say about you trying to convert people to the dark side for toasters."

Mack shook her head. "Beth, that's possibly...very sweet of you? But I don't try to convert anyone. You can't—" Mack stopped herself and shook her head. Beth wasn't the enemy here. She was just misinformed. And if she wasn't going to kick Mack out, then well, she had already won in this situation. "Never mind. Let's just try and study. Okay?"

Beth took the book, only to set it aside. She scooted a little closer to Mack, their knees almost touching. Her intense stare made Mack's throat close up.

"How did you know that you liked girls?"

If Mack had let herself, she would have clammed up right then and told Beth to back off. She didn't feel the need to defend her queerness to anyone, especially a girl who had just called her a sinner. But she bit her lip and saw Beth's eyes, big and trusting, and caved.

"I…don't know. I just did." She shrugged helplessly. "I just knew I…felt it. I never felt the same things for boys that I felt for girls. I didn't stare at their lips or want to touch their hair or any of that creepy teenage stuff I want to do with girls. You know?"

Beth nodded slowly, her face tight with concentration.

"Have you ever kissed a girl before?"

Mack felt her entire face heat up from embarrassment and she said quietly. "No."

"Do you want to?"

Mack let out a humorless chuckle. "Of course I do. But no girl wants to kiss me."

She looked back at Beth who was just staring at her. She'd scooted a little closer to Mack and Mack's palms started to sweat.

"Can I kiss you?" Beth asked softly.

Mack's heart felt like it was about to beat out of her chest. Beth was so close now that she could smell her perfume and it was making her dizzy. Did Beth always smell this good? Like flowers and candy? She supposed she'd never been close enough to her to find out. Just like she'd never been close enough to notice how her hazel eyes had flecks of gold in them and her mouth curved so prettily.

She felt herself blush when she realized she was just staring at Beth's lips and shook her head. "A-aren't you afraid you're going to catch my gay? Or whatever it is that they say?"

She kicked herself for not just saying yes. The only thing she could think about was how sweaty her armpits felt. Could Beth tell she was sweating through her shirt?

Beth shrugged. "I think I may have already caught it. A long time ago."

Mack swallowed thickly. "Oh."

Her brain short circuited with the combination of Beth's confession and how close she was. She felt hands cover her knees as Beth leaned even closer to her. Mack's eyes darted around Beth's face, looking for any sign that this was some cruel joke. Her hands were warm and soft. Mack could tell even through her jeans. Her breath tickled Mack's lips and she licked them nervously.

Beth leaned forward and their lips touched in a chaste kiss that couldn't have lasted more than a few seconds. But Mack was sure her heart exploded. She saw stars in front of her eyes. Were all girls' lips that soft? Or just Beth's? Even after Beth pulled away, Mack kept her eyes closed, her brain barely functioning.

"Wow," Mack breathed, finally opening her eyes. Beth was still close, a smile taking over her whole face. Oh no, she had dimples. Mack had the overwhelming desire to fall into them.

"That was so much nicer than kissing boys," Beth beamed. Without warning she crawled into Mack's lap sideways, arms around Mack's neck. Her hands naturally settled on Beth's hips, fingers playing nervously with the thin fabric of her T-shirt. Mack wondered if this was a dream. A pretty girl—a *cheerleader*— in her lap, saying how kissing her was better than kissing boys.

"Yeah," Mack agreed, eyes darting between Beth's lips and eyes. The gentle weight on Mack's lap made her stomach churn in a not completely unpleasant way.

Beth pulled her lip between her teeth and Mack felt her breath catch in her throat. "I want to keep kissing you," Beth whispered, brushing their noses together. Mack nodded— perhaps too eagerly—and leaned in again, but Beth pulled back a little. "You just can't tell anyone."

"Okay," Mack agreed easily. Beth ducked her head and connected their lips again, fingers playing with the hair at the back of Mack's neck. She sighed and wrapped her arms completely around Beth as they kissed...hoping it wasn't all a dream.

Somewhere in the back of her mind, it bothered Mack that Beth didn't want her to tell anyone. She couldn't say she was surprised. She didn't think that anyone would be super excited to tell the world that they had kissed...*Mackenzie Gomez*. But she figured she had no one to tell besides Lila anyways so who cared? And Lila fell under the "best friend" clause which meant that agreements like this didn't count if Mack told her. Mack wondered if maybe there was something more to it. Something she should ask about. But then she felt Beth's tongue ghost her bottom lip and all rational thoughts flew out of her head as she leaned in.

CHAPTER SIX

Finally Mack knew what it felt like, *really* knew what it felt like to be like one of the cool kids in the movies, walking down the hall in slow motion. She had woken up with a smile on her face, lips still tingling from the night before. She danced and sang as she got ready for school and now as she walked through the halls, sunglasses over her eyes, Mack didn't care who was looking at her or whispering about her.

She had kissed a girl. A pretty girl. A *cheerleader*.

Something Mack had never thought would happen had finally happened. And it exceeded her expectations completely.

Beth's lips were so soft and she tasted like candy. And she was so warm. Mack remembered tentatively tracing Beth's curves with her hands and felt a surge of pride. Mack's head was held high and she had a smirk on her face that couldn't be wiped away.

She nodded at a girl who glanced at her until she ran into someone, sunglasses falling off her nose. Mack stumbled and looked up to see Lila standing in front of her.

"Why do you look so smug?" she asked, looking Mack up and down. Mack was at Beth's way past curfew the night before and had to keep herself from calling Lila as soon as she left her house. But she wanted to see the look on her face when she told her what went down. Mack pushed her sunglasses on top of her head, her grin widening as they continued to their lockers.

"You were right about Beth," Mack said twirling the lock to her locker.

Lila hit Mack's arm hard, mouth open in excitement. "I knew it! She's gayer than Kristen Stewart!"

Mack shushed her and looked around to make sure no one was listening in. When she was satisfied, she put her books back in her locker. She couldn't help the smile that tugged on her lips when she put her English book away.

"You totally hooked up with her, didn't you? That's why you didn't answer my texts last night," Lila whispered, eyebrows wiggling. Mack nodded and Lila squealed, leaning against the lockers. "How was it?"

Mack sighed dreamily, "It was…nice. Actually. Beth is really sweet and I like hanging out with her."

She watched as Lila's face fell a little. "Wait. You actually *like* her?"

Mack shifted self-consciously. "Well…not like *that*. I think." She paused for a moment. Did she like Beth? No. She had barely spoken to her before last night. There was a small pull in her belly when she thought of her but…no. "I don't know. We could be good friends I think. Friends that…make out." She shrugged, trying to play it off, even as she felt her stomach flutter at the thought of kissing Beth again.

"Is that weird?"

Lila looked at her for a moment before shaking her head. "Um. No. Not weird."

Mack had been looking forward to English class all day. It was the only class she had with Beth and she'd only seen her briefly during the day. When she did it was always just as one of them was going into a classroom and they couldn't even chance a glance at each other.

But Beth was already sitting in her seat when Mack got to the classroom. Her heart fluttered as she slid into her seat next to Beth.

"Hey," Beth said softly with a shy smile.

"Hey," Mack said breathily.

Ms. Inkelbam stood at the front of the classroom and the chatter died down as she began to teach. Mack kept glancing over at Beth every few seconds, their eyes meeting. Beth hunched over her desk for a minute and straightened up. She waited for the teacher's back to be turned and held her hand out toward Mack, who hesitated a moment before reaching over and taking Beth's hand. She took the crumpled piece of paper Beth held, tingles running all the way up her arm just from the simple touch of their fingers.

Hey. :)

Just the simple word made Mack's stomach flip. She'd never written a note to a girl before. Not in this way. Mack leaned forward and responded.

Hey. I had fun last night. :)

She passed the note back quickly and Beth passed it back after responding.

Me too. I told Meghan we made out.

Mack felt herself panic when she read it and looked up at Beth, but she was just looking straight ahead at the board. She quickly scribbled back a response.

What did she say?

She said I probably caught the gay and should go to confession about it. I told her that wasn't possible because she would have caught the gay from her bf who I totally saw making out with the janitor. Then she threatened my Beanie Baby collection. So she's a hippo.

Mack blinked at the letter as she tried to sort through everything that Beth had said. She quickly scribbled back.

A hippo? Like the animal?

No like a hippo. Someone who says one thing and does another.

Mack chuckled to herself. *Hypocrite.* God, Beth was cute.

Well I'll make sure she doesn't get to your Beanie Baby collection. ;)

That's sweet. Thank you. :) They're insured like Mariah Carey's legs.

Mack snorted in laughter and tried to hide it behind her hand. She looked over to where Lila was staring at her with a frown. Mack just shrugged and went back to the note.

I bet they're worth more than her legs.

Mack rolled her eyes at herself as she passed the note. She needed to get better at this…flirting thing. If that's what she was doing. Were they flirting? Was she flirting with a girl? In class? Her suspicions were confirmed when Beth wrote her back.

Can we meet under the bleachers? At lunch?

Yeah. :)

Mack bit her lip and slid down into her seat with giddiness. Something in the back of her mind told her these feelings, the way her heart would flutter, wasn't normal for just a friend thing. But she was sure it had everything to do with Beth being the first girl she kissed. Things would calm down the more girls she kissed. She was sure of it.

"You were passing notes with Beth in class? The ancient version of texting?" Lila asked as they put their books in the locker.

Mack cleared her throat and shrugged. "Yeah. We're friends," she said nonchalantly, "We're meeting at lunch."

"Guess I'll just eat by myself then. Or just watch you two make out under the bleachers."

Mack cringed and put her hand on Lila's arm. "I'm sorry. I'll make it up to you. Okay?"

Lila rolled her eyes and continued putting things in her locker without even a glance at Mack.

"*Top Model* rewatch tonight while eating shitty pizza?" Mack asked with a smile.

Lila finally looked at Mack and sighed. "Fine."

"Thank you!" Mack hugged Lila briefly before adjusting the backpack on her shoulder. "I'll see you after lunch."

She walked out of the school and tried to look as casual as possible ducking behind the bleachers. Beth wasn't there yet so Mack set her backpack on the ground and leaned against a pole. She wanted to look as cool as possible. But nonchalant. Like she wasn't trying to be cool, so leaning seemed like the best option.

She had just arranged herself against the pole when Beth rounded the corner and appeared under the bleachers. Mack smiled widely before slipping off the pole and hitting her head.

"Ow! Shit," she said, cheeks heating as she rubbed the growing lump on the side of her head.

Beth, clearly holding back a smile, bit down on her lip. "Are you okay?"

"I am now," she said reaching for Beth's hand. She mentally patted herself on the back and entwined their fingers together. Beth blushed a little and Mack counted that as a win. She took a deep breath; the overwhelming urge to kiss Beth was becoming too much. She looked around to make sure no one was watching before she pressed a kiss to Beth's lips. But she got cheek instead. When she opened her eyes, Beth was looking down with trepidation written all over her face.

Mack's entire face heated and she shook her head. "What's wrong? I'm sorry," she said letting go of Beth's hand. "I...Is it my breath?" She breathed into her palm to smell her breath, but Beth took her hand back before she could determine if that was a factor in Beth's rejection.

"Your breath is lovely," Beth sighed. "It's not that. I just... have some things I need to figure out."

Mack squeezed Beth's hand and took a step closer. "Is everything okay?" Beth nodded and Mack ducked her head to catch Beth's eye. "Does it have to do with your Beanie Babies?"

Beth put her hand over her heart. "No, thank goodness. I'm just...confused."

Mack felt dread spreading through her stomach. "Is it... Does it have to do with kissing me?"

With a shuddery sigh, Beth nodded. Mack should have known. She should have expected this. It was a fluke getting to kiss Beth. Her brain searched for something to say. She thought back to when she finally realized she was gay and what she wished someone had said to her.

"It's okay. You're probably going through gay panic," Mack said calmly. "It's totally normal. I went through it a few years ago and tried to convince myself I had a thing for Justin Bieber." Mack paused for a second and frowned. "Looking back that was probably one of the gayest things I could have done."

Beth giggled and put a single finger over Mack's lips to stop her from rambling. She smiled against Beth's fingertip. It felt so soft and so...intimate. Just a simple gesture. Mack wanted to gather Beth into her arms, but she was going to follow Beth's lead on what kind of touching was okay right now. Plus she was sure that Beth would be able to feel the way her heart hammered against her ribs.

"I promise you this has nothing to do with Justin Bieber."

"Then what is it?" Mack asked as Beth's finger fell from her lips and played with the gold cross around her own neck.

"I just have some things to think about. Reflect on. You know?" Beth's eyes remained glued to a random spot behind Mack. She took Beth's hand away from her necklace and gently pulled it down to her side, hoping to get her attention again.

"Is there anything I can do to help?" Mack asked with a hopeful smile. "I've kind of been through this whole, 'oh shit, I'm gay' thing before."

"It's not just about being gay. It's about...well...the things they said in the assembly the other day. I just started thinking about it after last night while I was reading Dickinson. You know, I actually kind of like her."

Mack felt like she'd been dunked in cold water and quickly dropped both of Beth's hands like she'd been burned. Right. The assembly. This entire fucking school that told her and everyone else that being gay wasn't okay. That it was a choice you were supposed to ignore despite your heart. She didn't know why she'd thought Beth would be immune.

She was so distracted she couldn't even spend time registering that Beth actually read the homework.

"Oh, right," Mack said, picking at the skin on her thumb.

Beth quickly took Mack's hand back. "I'm not going to turn on you. If that's what you think."

"But Father Jorge—"

"He has his beliefs. It doesn't mean they're mine," Beth said firmly. "I need to talk to Jesus and come to my own decisions."

Mack shifted uncomfortably and muttered under her breath. "If you're talking to Jesus, I'm pretty sure I know where that conversation is going to go."

"Hey," Beth tugged Mack's hand, and Mack stumbled forward a little. Beth put her hand on Mack's cheek and caught her eyes. She placed a gentle kiss on her other cheek with a smile. "Don't worry about it. Okay? You're still the nicest and best kisser I've ever met."

Mack couldn't help the pride that inflated her chest, reaching up to her mouth and planting a cocky smile there. Just the simple kiss made all of her worries melt away. Beth wasn't going to turn on her. And for whatever reason, Mack believed her. Beth was a lot of things, but Mack never pegged her for a dishonest person.

"Yeah, well," Mack said through her smile, "it can only get better."

Beth rolled her eyes, "You're making it really hard not to kiss you right now."

"Maybe that's the point."

Beth frowned good naturedly before kissing the corner of her mouth. "Let's go back to the cafeteria. They have tater tots today."

Mack found herself daydreaming in History class. How could she not? She tried to focus on her notes about the Black Plague but her mind kept wandering to Beth. The slide on the board changed to a close up of a bloated leech and Mack snapped out of her daydream with a cringe.

"Bloodletting was a device often used in this time to drain a patient of their ailments," the teacher droned as people took notes.

Mack had a nagging feeling someone was looking at her and turned around to see Meghan staring at her. She was twirling her ponytail around her finger and frowning at Mack like she was trying to figure something out. Mack shifted uncomfortably and turned back to the front of the classroom with an unpleasant shiver.

She kept finding reasons to look over her shoulder, and every time Meghan was staring at her. Mack wondered if there was some kind of hit put out on her. Mack packed her bag before the bell rang, ready to run out of the classroom as soon as they were dismissed to avoid Meghan. The last thing she needed was to be cornered.

The bell rang and Mack leaped up from her seat before it even ended. She was the first one out of the classroom and she sighed, relieved. She opened her locker and was getting her books for the rest of the day when—

"Hey."

Mack jumped about a foot in the air, hand on her chest where her heart threatened to escape. Meghan was standing next to her, perfectly sculpted eyebrow raised into her hairline. It felt like she was a foot taller than Mack.

"How the fuck did you get here so fast?" Mack gasped.

"Language," Meghan chastised as if she were bored. She looked down at her nails briefly before looking back up at Mack. "I need you to come over tonight."

Mack blinked at her for a moment. "What?"

Meghan rolled her eyes and crossed her arms over her chest. "Listen. I need you to bloodlet me."

"That's illegal," Mack squawked. "I'm not a licensed doctor."

"Not literally, dumbass. I..." She rolled her eyes again and said quickly, "I kissed a girl at Chad's party last week, and I need you to kiss me again to get rid of the gay."

Mack frowned, "That makes no—"

"It makes perfect sense. We just learned about it. It's like one cancels the other out. At least that's what Josh said."

"Josh? Your clearly homosexual boyfriend?" Mack said incredulously.

"He's not gay."

Mack held her hands up in surrender and shrugged. "Why me?"

"Look around. You see any other lesbians hanging around? Plus, I thought you wanted to like...kiss all the cheerleaders or whatever."

Mack sighed and shifted uncomfortably. She did have a point. Mack had forgotten about her plan as soon as Beth had kissed her and here Meghan was basically offering herself on a silver platter.

"Um...okay," Mack said with a shrug, trying to look more confident than she felt. "I'll be there at six."

"Seven," Meghan said before walking away. Mack watched her for a moment, eyes wandering down to watch Meghan's hips as she left.

"What was that about?" Lila asked. Mack turned to her and shrugged.

"I guess I have a sort-of date with Meghan tonight."

Lila shook her head. "So no hanging out tonight?"

Mack cringed. "No. I'm sorry. But this is good, right? Part of the plan. It's finally coming together!"

Lila smiled tightly and slammed her locker shut. "Yeah. It's all coming together."

Mack changed her clothes when she got home and went through the routine of splashing water under her arms and brushing her hair and teeth. She got to Meghan's right at seven and the cheerleader ushered her into her room like she was smuggling something in. Mack stood at the doorway of her bedroom and looked around. For someone so frightening, her bedroom was fairly normal, though Mack wasn't sure what she was expecting.

Mack hit the side of her thighs with her hands awkwardly as she looked around. Meghan went to her closet and pointed vaguely at the bed. Mack sat down on the edge, hands fiddling nervously in her lap.

Meghan came out from her closet and marched over to Mack. Her eyes got wider as Meghan approached, heart beating uncontrollably as she came to a stop in front of her. Meghan's thighs bumped Mack's knees and an excitement started low in her belly, slowly taking over the fear.

"I have to kiss you now," Meghan said with a bored sigh. She held Mack's face between her hands and squashed it. Mack blinked up at her, waiting for Meghan to make the move. Without warning she surged forward until her face was a hair's breadth away.

Suddenly Meghan's eyes got wide and she pulled away. "I can't do this. This is ridiculous. I mean, you're wearing white after Labor Day! Who does that?"

Mack looked down at her white shirt and shook her head. "I'm not…It's not *that* bad."

"You're so convincing."

"I guarantee you I'm the best kisser you'll ever have the pleasure of encountering," Mack said, unsure of where her surge of newfound confidence came from. Probably from the fact that she was so ready to kiss another girl—even if that girl was Meghan, who terrified her.

Meghan frowned. "Why should I believe you? Why should I kiss you?"

Mack thought for a moment, licking her lips. "Because… because you want something from me. And I want something from you. It's just mutually beneficial. I won't tell anyone this happened."

Meghan studied Mack for a moment and she squirmed under her gaze. She put a firm hand on Mack's chest and pushed her back so that she bounced against the mattress. Meghan climbed onto the bed and straddled Mack. It felt like all the air left her lungs.

"What?"

"I need you to bloodlet me," Meghan said, her face so close their noses were touching. "Make me bleed out the gay."

"O-okay," Mack said resting her hands on Meghan's hips. Suddenly she pulled back again.

"Are you kissing anyone else?"

Mack flushed, stomach twisting uncomfortably and she thought of Beth. Funny, sweet and sexy Beth. "Um…no. Why?"

"Because the bloodletting wouldn't work if you were. You'd just be replenishing the gay."

Mack frowned as she tried to follow Meghan's reasoning, but it didn't matter when Meghan leaned down and connected their lips.

Mack's entire body felt like it was on fire in the most pleasant way, tingles going all the way down to her toes. Her hands tightened on Meghan's hips and all thoughts of Beth and Meghan's motivations flew out of her mind.

CHAPTER SEVEN

Mack felt like she was walking on air. In a week she had gone from being a closeted queer who had never kissed a girl to an out girl—no, *woman*—who had made out with *two* girls, both cheerleaders and both very hot. Even if one was terrifying and the other was...Beth. Sweet Beth. Just thinking of her made Mack's stomach ache, but she wasn't sure if that was a good thing or not.

She had gone to the mall a couple of nights before to get some new clothes. All the money she had saved up from chores and birthdays was finally coming in handy. To Mack, "saving up" usually just meant doing her usual thing of doing nothing except for the occasional movie with Lila. But now she had nice shirts that actually fit, and she made an effort not to wear the same pants every day for a week like she usually did.

Mack's confidence was at an all-time high. Was this what normal high school kids felt like? Confident and happy? She wondered how long it would last.

As she walked past the janitor's closet, a hand reached out, grabbed her arm and pulled her in. Mack felt her heart leap in her throat as she blinked in the darkness. It was finally happening. She was going to be murdered in a small dark space like her mother always warned her.

"I know karate!" Mack yelled, throwing up her hands in some sort of karate stance she once had seen on television.

"Do you really?" Beth whispered.

Mack blinked a few more times until she made out the outline of Beth crammed into the closet with her. She let out a soft sigh and dropped her hands in front of her.

"No," Mack confessed, "I was just thinking it might deter someone from trying to murder me."

Beth giggled and Mack felt goosebumps rise on her skin.

"You're funny," Beth said taking both of Mack's hands in her own and settling them onto her hips. Mack licked her lips nervously as Beth's hands trailed up her arms and over her shoulders.

"Thanks," Mack said softly with a lopsided grin. Her hands flexed against Beth's hips as she pulled her just a little closer. Beth surged forward, kissing Mack hard. Mack hummed in surprise and pulled away, despite herself. She wanted nothing more than to keep kissing Beth.

"I thought you said we couldn't kiss anymore? I don't want to mess up your journey with Jesus. Or whatever."

Beth smiled shyly and pushed some of Mack's hair behind her ear. "You're sweet."

"I try," Mack said lamely.

"I've been thinking and praying," Beth said, slowly backing Mack up until her back hit the wall. "And I've realized that being gay and loving Jesus don't have to be mutually exclusive."

"No?" Mack tried not to be distracted by the movement of Beth's lips.

Beth shook her head. "Jesus loves everyone. Especially gay people. And he wants people to be happy. So if kissing girls makes me happy, well, I'm not hurting anyone. Not really."

"That's very…evolved of you."

"Thank you for calling me evolved. Makes me feel like a Pokémon or something," Beth said. Her head tilted adorably and Mack pulled her even closer. "Which Pokémon am I?"

"Whatever the cutest one is," Mack flirted. Beth's blush was apparent even in the low lighting and Mack smiled proudly. "So that means you can kiss girls now?"

Beth nodded. "I can kiss girls now."

"Then why are we wasting time?" Mack smiled before leaning in and reconnecting her lips with Beth's. They were still as soft and wonderful as Mack remembered. Her heart fluttered in her chest and her hands smoothed along the scratchy fabric of Beth's cheer uniform as she pulled their bodies closer. Feeling every curve of Beth's body against her made Mack lightheaded and she didn't know what to concentrate on.

"This is nice," Beth said between kisses.

"Mmm," Mack said, more interested in kissing than talking at the moment. She could hardly believe she was getting that "making out in a closet" high school moment.

"Want to hang out this weekend?"

"Definitely."

Mack rushed to her next class after the bell shocked her and Beth from their makeout session. She had slipped into her seat just in time to avoid a reprimand for being late, chest heaving. She looked over at Lila who looked confused as to why she was panting like she had just run a marathon.

"Beth," Mack whispered, wiggling her eyebrows at Lila.

A cloud seemed to pass over her friend's face and she quickly turned back to the board. Mack looked at her for a moment before the lesson began.

After class, she and Lila walked to their lockers together. Lila didn't ask anything about Beth and Mack didn't offer up any kind of information. It seemed unusual since Lila always wanted to know everything that was going on, but Mack was too distracted to think too much about it.

"Hey," Lila began as they got their books for the next class. "I have a bunch of daytime judge shows recorded at home. Want to come over and watch with me tomorrow?"

"I can't," Mack said with an apologetic smile that soon transformed into a smug one. "I'm hanging out with Beth all day."

"What do you even do with Beth? Besides the obvious."

"I think you'd like Beth a lot if you hung out with her," Mack said. "She's funny and likes a lot of the same shows we do. Like *Top Model* and that show about antiques—"

"What about the next day?"

Mack sucked air through her teeth and shook her head. "I'm with Meghan that day."

Lila crossed her arms and frowned. "Is there any day you can hang out with me?"

"I can't. I'm hanging out with Beth and Meghan all weekend. Like…all weekend," Mack said, unable to help the proud smile that lit up her features. "But maybe next weekend!" Lila barked out a short laugh as Mack continued. "Actually, I need your help getting Daphne," she said as they started toward gym class. "She's the next cheerleader on my list, and I think I have a plan."

"A plan?"

Mack gave her a serious look. "Yes. And it involves something we've never done before unless forced to."

"Running?"

"Worse. We have to be on separate teams in P.E."

"Well, shit," Lila said as they stepped up to their gym lockers. They were tucked into a corner away from everyone else getting changed for class. It was a strategy that Mack developed in eighth grade so they wouldn't have to undress in front of other people. Mack took off her shoes first before slipping her shirt off without much thought. Some hair fell over her face as her shirt came off and she tried to blow it out of her face.

"I need you to throw a dodgeball at Daphne and I'll save her," Mack said, quickly running a hand through her hair to get it out of her eyes. "She's such a drama queen in P.E."

Lila wasn't answering. Mack looked over at her to see her staring, face flushed, eyes wide and fixated on Mack's torso. Mack frowned and she tried to get her attention. "Lila!"

Lila's gaze shot back to Mack's face and both of them blushed crimson.

"What the fuck?" Mack asked with a shake of her head. "Are you not listening?"

"What?" Lila choked out, "Yes. Yeah. Throw a dodgeball at Daphne." She blinked and shook her head. "Have you been working out?"

"What? Don't you know me at all?"

"You have abs."

Mack frowned and looked down at her stomach. "Those aren't abs. Those are just like default abs because I don't eat right and my metabolism is at its peak."

"I...okay," Lila said shaking her head and turning back to her locker. She kept her back to Mack as she took her own shirt off. Mack shrugged her gym T-shirt on.

"Don't worry. My mom says I'm gonna start packing on the pounds at around nineteen like she did." Mack sighed as she slipped off her jeans to put on her gym shorts. "So are you going to help me with the plan?"

Lila looked at Mack like she was trying to figure out what she was talking about. She cleared her throat. "Um...yeah. Throw the dodgeball at Daphne or whatever."

Mack clapped her hands together in excitement and smiled at Lila. "Great! I can't wait."

Mack stood at the front of the pack for the first time in P.E. She remembered why she hated this class. Why she hated this *game*. The need to have teenagers lob balls at each other for a grade still baffled her, but she needed to be at the front for her plan to work. And she was determined for it to work.

They all stood on the basketball court, the middle line dividing the two teams. Lila stood on the other side of the line and Mack looked behind her to find Daphne. She spotted her standing on the sidelines chatting with another girl. Mack rolled her neck in anticipation, legs wide apart in a stance that seemed to her like it looked like she knew what she was doing.

The gym teacher blew the whistle and Mack made a show of being into the game. It was a delicate balance of not striking right away, but making sure that Daphne didn't get out before Lila could throw the ball at her.

When she finally felt like the timing was right, Mack made eye contact with Lila and nodded. Lila twirled the ball between her hands, something odd and hard flickering in her eyes. She wound up, hand cradling the ball far back behind her before she threw it over hand right at Daphne. Mack ran to interfere, sprinting toward Daphne and throwing herself in front of the ball. It hit her hard in the stomach and she felt the wind get knocked out of her. Mack crumpled to the ground, her stomach hurting as she gasped for breath.

"Oh my gosh. Are you okay?" Daphne said in an almost bored tone as she looked down at Mack. She made a show of opening her eyes slowly and groaning a little.

"I think I'll be okay," Mack said with a pathetic cough.

Lila stood over her, arms crossed. Mack saw her roll her eyes and walk off just as the gym teacher came over and offered Mack his hand. He hauled her up and Mack still held her stomach.

"Get off my court, Mackenzie," he said waving her toward the locker rooms. "Daphne, assist her please?"

Daphne shrugged and managed to look at least a little concerned as she walked with Mack over to the locker room.

She sat down on the bench and Daphne leaned against the lockers.

"Do you need like…ice?" Daphne asked.

Mack shook her head. "Thank you, though," she said with a strained smile.

"I'm sorry you took a ball to the stomach for me," Daphne said, sitting on the bench next to Mack with the barest hint of a smile. "It was nice of you."

Mack felt a surge of that newfound confidence fill her chest and she smiled at Daphne, leaning a little forward. "I couldn't let you get hit in that pretty face of yours."

Daphne stared at her for a moment before releasing what could have been either a giggle or a hiccup, Mack wasn't entirely sure, especially since Daphne's facial expression didn't change at all with the sound.

"Are you hitting on me?"

"Um…" Mack felt her confidence draining. "Maybe?"

"I'm straight."

"Right," Mack said, leaning back out of Daphne's face. "Sorry."

Daphne shrugged. "But Chad is a jerk and my boyfriend is a jerk too. So you can tell people we kissed if you do me a favor."

Mack just stared at Daphne, trying to figure out if she had actually just gotten that lucky.

"That's what you're trying to do, right? Get all the cheerleaders to kiss you?" Daphne said, going back to picking at her nails. "So if you help me with my project for woodshop you can tell people we like…kissed or whatever."

"You don't care?" Mack asked with a raised eyebrow.

Daphne shook her head, only looking at Mack briefly before going back to her nails. "Eh. I'm almost out of here anyway."

"Um, okay," Mack said with a shrug, still waiting for the other shoe to drop. "I don't really know a lot about woodworking, though."

"I thought lesbians were good with wood," Daphne stated.

Mack frowned but nodded slowly. "Sure."

"Wanna just stay in here until the end of gym class?" Daphne asked.

"Yes, please," Mack said breathing a sigh of relief as they both settled into a comfortable silence.

Lila had somehow managed to avoid Mack in the gym locker room. When Mack saw her at their lockers, she punched her in the arm. Lila jumped and grabbed her arm with a yell.

"Ow! What the fuck?" she said already aiming to retaliate but Mack dodged it.

"That's for hitting me so hard with that ball," Mack hissed at her.

Lila rolled her eyes. "Whatever. Baby. You told me to do it!"

"It worked too." Mack wiggled her eyebrows. "Well, in a way. She said I could tell everyone we kissed if I helped her with a project for her woodworking class."

"That's weird."

"I know."

"Also you know nothing about woodworking."

"Minor detail," Mack said with a dismissive wave. "I'm hoping it's like an instinctive lesbian thing."

"Idiot. I hope you get a splinter."

"Ha ha," Mack said sarcastically. "It's going to be fine. I'll call you about it later."

"I'll be waiting with bated breath," Lila said flatly as they parted ways for their next class.

Mack sat cross legged on the cold garage floor, her head cocked to the side as she tried to determine where to go from here. The block of wood sat silently in front of her just as unhelpfully as it had a few moments ago. She looked over at Daphne who was sitting on an old car bench seat against the wall, reading a magazine.

"So...I don't know if I can make this into a canoe," Mack said looking back at the piece of wood that was about as big as her forearm.

"I believe in you," Daphne answered, staring at her magazine, clearly only half listening.

Mack ran a hand through her hair and looked back at the wood. She took a deep breath and picked up the X-acto knife.

"Guess I'll just hope for the best," she muttered under her breath as she began to hack away at the block. It was a good thing getting all these cheerleaders was worth it or she might have thrown in the towel a long time ago. But she thought about the look on Chad's face when she told him which cheerleaders she'd kissed. That. That would make all this worth it.

* * *

Mack sat in her English class waiting for Lila. She hadn't answered any of her calls or texts the night before, after she left Daphne's. Through some sort of lesbian miracle, she had managed to turn the block of wood into the vague shape of a canoe but she wasn't done. Her fingers were covered with bandages from where she'd repeatedly stabbed herself with the knife.

Just before the bell rang, Lila slipped into the seat next to Mack. She looked incredulously at Lila, who just stared straight ahead. Mack waved her hand to get Lila's attention and she turned to her with an apologetic smile. She breathed a small sigh of relief to at least see Lila acknowledging her.

"I tried calling you last night," Mack said as she played with the corner of her notebook.

"Sorry. I was busy." Lila finished. Mack felt Lila watching her curl the paper a moment before looking back at her. "Actually, I was thinking. Can we...I want to talk about this whole you making out with cheerleaders thing."

Mack frowned and felt her stomach twist at the look on her friend's face. "Um...sure. What is it?"

Lila scooted her desk a little closer to Mack's and sighed. Mack looked at her intently just as her phone buzzed in her pocket. Out of instinct she took it out, hiding it from the teacher under the table as she read Beth's name on the screen. She smiled to herself and opened the text as Lila started talking.

"I don't know. I guess I've just been having weird feelings lately that I don't know how to deal with," Lila mumbled.

Mack hummed in acknowledgement, half listening as she read the text.

Beth: Hey hot stuff. Wanna help me with these vocab words ;)

Mack felt herself flush and looked up at Beth, Lila's talking droning on somewhere in the distance. Suddenly she only had a one-track mind and all she could think of were Beth's lips on her own and how her curves felt under her hands. Beth waved at her from her desk, smiling and winking at Mack. If possible, her cheeks got even redder when Beth crossed her legs at the thigh and her already short skirt exposed more of her legs.

"Mack...*Mack*."

Lila hit her shoulder and Mack jumped, hitting her knee on the underside of her desk. She hissed in pain as she looked over at Lila who had questions written all over her face.

"What?" Mack asked before remembering Lila had been talking to her. "I'm sorry I just...um...distracted."

"Did you hear anything I said?" Lila asked, hurt lacing the angry quiver of her voice.

Mack cringed a little. "I'm really sorry, I am. But I have to help Beth with something. We can talk later. Okay? I promise."

Lila just leaned back in her chair. "Fine. Whatever."

Mack stood up from her desk eagerly, gathered all her stuff and filled the seat in front of Beth. Beth practically beamed at her and Mack smiled back, turning around and folding her arms on Beth's desk.

"So, I heard you need help," Mack said softly.

Beth pointed to the first question on her homework. "You don't mind?"

"I'm always down to help a damsel in distress," Mack said with the crooked smile that always made Beth blush. She didn't know why. It was the same smile that Suzan had told her in their freshman year made her look like she had a stroke. But Beth liked it and that was good enough for Mack.

Beth's eyes darted over to Lila for a moment before looking back down at her paper. "So like, Lila has a crush on you," she said simply.

Mack stared at Beth for a moment before letting out a short snort of laughter. "No, she doesn't."

"Are you sure?" Beth asked as she looked at Mack. She lost herself in hazel eyes for a moment before shaking herself out of them. Mack was still at a loss for why Beth had this weird effect on her. Like she had tunnel vision just for her and everything came out in stupid when she talked to her. Maybe it was because Beth was the first girl she kissed. Her mom had always said the first person you kissed was special, even if it didn't mean anything.

"I'm pretty positive," Mack said with a nod. "We've been best friends for like…ever."

Beth looked over at Lila again and back to Mack. "Do *you* have a crush on *her*?"

"No," Mack said quickly—almost too quickly, even for her own liking. Beth raised an eyebrow but nodded.

"Okay," Beth said letting her fingers brush over the top of Mack's hand ever so briefly. Electricity shot up Mack's arm, hair standing on end as she cleared her throat. "So, help me with my homework?"

Mack had never been so eager to do someone else's homework in her life.

CHAPTER EIGHT

Mack wondered how many years of good karma she was getting paid back for right now. Was it the time she rescued some baby kittens from a dumpster and took them home? Then got the worst ringworm right on her neck and got shit for it at school for at least a month? That had to be worth at least one month of good luck.

That must be how she ended up here, lying on Beth's bed with their lips attached. They were facing each other, Beth's hands up the back of Mack's shirt while her own were wandering up and down Beth's sides. Every few minutes she'd get brave and let her hand graze the side of Beth's breast over her shirt or her hands would roam down to the swell of her ass. But Mack kept it very respectable. Mostly because she was sure she would combust if her hands wandered any further.

Believe it or not, the night had started innocently enough. Beth had a surprisingly large collection of video games that she and Mack had nerded out over. How their very innocent two-person shooting game had turned into an intense makeout session, Mack wasn't sure. But she certainly wasn't going to complain.

It felt like every time they hung out, Mack learned something new and interesting about Beth. Part of her wished she had started talking to her sooner. And not just because she really *really* liked kissing her.

"You taste like peanut butter," Beth whispered as she kissed across Mack's cheek and down her neck. Mack frowned but the feeling of Beth's lips on her neck made all the questions she had fly out of her mind. Goosebumps erupted over her skin and her grip tightened on Beth's hips.

She felt her phone buzzing in her pocket but ignored it. It buzzed again and Mack groaned in annoyance. She took it out to turn it off but saw a text from Daphne and quickly opened it, Beth's lips still attached to her neck.

Hey. Come over and hang out.

Mack's heart jumped and she thought for a moment. She didn't want to leave Beth, especially with whatever it was she was doing with her lips right now. But she also didn't want to piss off Daphne in any way or else she might spill the beans about them never actually kissing.

"Babe—I mean, uh, Beth," Mack said, quickly correcting herself and hoping her face wasn't as red as it felt. "I have to go."

Beth pulled away, either not catching Mack's slip up or not caring. But she looked at her with those big eyes, lips slightly swollen. Mack hated that look because it made her stomach clench every time.

"Wait, why?" Beth asked. Mack brushed some hair behind Beth's ear and smiled awkwardly.

"I have to go. My mom needs help with dinner," she said before sitting up. Beth sighed, turning to watch Mack as she slipped her boots back on.

"Aw, that's sweet," Beth smiled.

Mack felt guilt settle in her stomach but sent off a quick reply text to Daphne anyway, saying she was on the way. Mack frowned when she felt how chapped her lips were.

"Can I ask you a question?" Beth asked, her voice small and vulnerable.

Mack immediately stopped lacing her boots and sat up on the bed. "Of course."

Beth smiled and pulled Mack's hand into her lap. "I know your original plan was to kiss a bunch of cheerleaders but…are you?"

Her mouth ran dry. Really, she should have been expecting this question. "Am I what?"

"Kissing other cheerleaders," Beth already looked on the verge of tears.

Mack couldn't bring herself to hurt Beth, so instead she just forced a smile. There was no way Beth would find out the truth anyway. Meghan certainly didn't want people to know they were kissing, and Mack could cut that off at any time. After this weekend, she reasoned, she would only kiss Beth. So instead of telling the truth, Mack just avoided it.

"You're the only girl I want to kiss, Beth," Mack deflected, leaning down to kiss her again.

Beth's smile was blinding and she tried to pull Mack back down onto the bed, but she managed to pull away.

"Do you have any Chapstick?" Mack asked. Beth threw herself on her stomach to reach into her side drawer. She held up a tube triumphantly and sat back to hand it to Mack. Dr. Pepper Lip Smackers. Mack smiled and took it. "Thank you."

Mack put some on her lips and Beth stood. She gripped Mack's collar and pulled her forward, planting one last firm kiss on her lips and leaving Mack dazed. Beth pulled away slowly, a lazy smile spreading across her face.

"Dr. Pepper is my favorite," Beth said.

Mack swallowed thickly, licking her lips and nodding. "Y-yeah. I'll text you?"

"Please," Beth said, sitting back on her bed as Mack walked out the door.

* * *

The next morning, Mack walked into school taking a long swig from the giant water bottle she had grabbed on her way out the door. Her mouth felt dry and she smirked to herself. The weekend had been spent juggling Beth and Daphne and Meghan. Sure with Daphne there was no actual making out involved, just another weird woodworking project, but it was still tiring. Wonderfully so. But still.

As she walked down the hall, she saw Lila at her locker and practically skipped up to her. She leaned against her own locker, smirking at her friend. If anyone would appreciate her activities that weekend, it would be Lila.

"Hey," Mack said, "Sorry I couldn't answer your calls over the weekend. I was so busy with Beth and Daphne...and Meghan. Gosh." Mack tipped the water bottle back and took a long sip as she shrugged. "I think I'm dehydrated. Like, seriously. I lost so much spit over the weekend."

Lila rolled her eyes so hard, Mack was surprised she didn't strain something. She frowned and kicked Lila's shoe lightly to get her attention but Lila just sighed dramatically.

"Mack, I don't have time to talk," she said closing her locker and finally gracing Mack with a glance. "I have to be somewhere. Excuse me."

Lila pushed unnecessarily past Mack who just stood there blinking, mind trying to catch up with what just had happened. She hadn't heard Lila talk to her like that since the fourth grade when she got mad that Mack won the spelling bee and she didn't. Mack turned and followed her.

"Wait, where are you going?" she asked as she caught up with her.

Lila faced her dramatically, a sigh leaving her lips as she flipped her hair over her shoulder. "If you must know, I've become a cheerleader."

Mack stared at Lila for a moment just as she walked away again. Still, Mack stood and stared where Lila had been standing before her weird announcement. There was no way. She must have misheard her. Mack ran after her.

"You're kidding," Mack said with a sarcastic laugh. "There's no way you became a *cheerleader*. You can hardly get out of bed without tripping! Can you even use pompoms without punching yourself in the face?"

Lila spun around, anger on her face. Mack almost ran into her with the sudden stop, eyes wide as she looked up.

"You know I used to be a baton twirler," Lila said, waving her arms dramatically.

"Yeah, until you tried to do a triple-axle back wrist twist and gave yourself a concussion."

Lila blushed, stomping her foot angrily. "You know it was humid that day. My baton was slippery! Plus, what do you expect me to do? Huh? It seems like you only have time for cheerleaders these days."

Her voice broke a little and Mack stuttered in disbelief. To say she felt taken aback would be an understatement. She felt anger rise up in her chest and she shook her head.

"You know that's not true."

"Isn't it? You're so busy trying to get into their Spankies that you hardly give me the time of day anymore."

"That's not true," Mack growled in frustration and she ran a hand through her hair. "I— How did you even get on the team? They're not having tryouts right now."

Mack watched as Lila's face fell for a moment. She could practically see the wheels spinning in her head as she looked away for a moment and back at Mack. She sighed and crossed her arms.

"Well, I'm not necessarily a cheerleader," Lila said softly, eyes finding an interesting spot on the ceiling. "I'm the towel girl. But I still get to go to Nationals and I still get a T-shirt."

Lila spun on her heels, nodded once firmly, and walked toward the girls' locker room.

Mack followed again, sputtering and trying to find her words. "You're being ridiculous!"

She knew she'd made a mistake as soon as Lila turned toward her again, eyes wide and angry as she pointed at herself. "Me? *I'm* being ridiculous? Ha!" Lila pushed her finger roughly into the middle of Mack's chest, sending her stumbling back. "That's rich coming from the girl who spends all her time making out with the same cheerleaders you used to make fun of!"

Mack pushed Lila's hand away and poked her in middle of her chest in retaliation, backing her up toward the lockers as she spoke. "Listen, *you're* the one who encouraged this!" Mack said before taking on a mocking tone. "Oh, 'steal all the football players' girlfriends,' you said. Now look what happened! You're getting all butt hurt and tried to fix it by volunteering to take these girls' sweaty towels!"

Lila's back hit the lockers and she snarled, pushing Mack away from her. But Mack didn't move. She held her ground even as Lila yelled back at her.

"Well I'm sorry I was trying to be a good friend by encouraging you to have some confidence for once. And it's not like I actually thought you would get your head out of your ass long enough to make yourself look presentable and actually get a girl at all. Let alone a cheerleader."

Mack flinched a little, hurt. Lila's words stung more than she thought they would. All of her insecurities bubbled to the surface, doubt once again seeping into her brain as she tried to think of a response. All she wanted to do was push Lila and go cry in a corner somewhere. But she bit back her tears and tried to seem unaffected instead.

"You know what? Screw you," Mack said, hating how her voice cracked as she backed away from Lila, who stomped over to a bin of dirty towels, gripping the edge and frowning at Mack.

"Screw *you!*" Lila replied.

"Enjoy not being able to wash the smell of mediocre athleticism off." Mack shouted, walking out.

Lila pulled two dirty towels from the bin and used them like pompoms as she yelled, "Ra, ra, fuck you, jerk!"

Mack stormed away, tears still stinging behind her eyes. She decided spending her next class in the bathroom would be better.

Mack managed to drag herself through the first half of classes, avoiding Lila as much as possible. She allowed herself one angry cry and then proceeded with her day. Her chest felt empty and she hated that she actually *missed* Lila. It had been, what? Four hours? She was fucking pathetic.

Before lunch, Mack found herself at her locker. Beth appeared beside her, seemingly out of nowhere and she felt her heart lift a little bit. She smiled softly at the other girl as she put her books in her locker.

"Hey," Mack said.

"Hey there, secret girlfriend," Beth said with a small wink.

Mack felt her heart skip before realization hit her and it immediately sunk. *Girlfriend?* Since...when? If they were girlfriends, there was a whole lot that Mack already fucked up on. Mostly the kissing other girls thing.

"So are we coordinating for prom?" Beth continued, not noticing Mack's wide eyes and shocked face.

"I um..." Mack shook her head, hoping some clarity would come with that but nothing. "I uh, thought we were supposed to be a secret?"

Beth bounced a little in excitement while Mack's panic only grew. "That's why I'm a genius."

She pointed proudly to the button on her chest and Mack looked down. The button was huge, probably because there was so much writing shoved onto the little metal disk.

Friends of LGBTQ (but only friends and definitely not gay) Club

"Wow," Mack said flatly. "That's very specific."

"I'm a genius, right?" Beth wiggled her eyebrows. "As the president of this newly formed club, I want to make a statement. And what would make a better statement than going to prom with the most popular and only out lesbian at school?"

Mack chuckled and shook her head. "I'm not popular, Beth."

"Of course you are, silly," Beth said hitting her arm lightly. "You're popular because you're gay."

"I hardly call that popular. I'd say it makes me more notorious than anything." Mack closed her locker and turned toward Beth. She looked so sweet and hopeful. The last thing Mack wanted to do was to disappoint her. Mack wanted to protect her at all costs. But then Mack remembered what Lila had said earlier. She was just a nothing girl who barely got her head out of her ass long enough to change her appearance. Mack wasn't good enough for Beth. Clearly. "I think you should go with someone else. Someone who's *actually* popular."

Beth's face fell and Mack almost instantly regretted saying it.

"But…why? I wanna go with you."

Mack pushed some hair from her face and shook her head. "Beth, if you go with me, it could ruin your reputation. Do you want people talking about you behind your back?"

Beth shook her head and took a step closer to Mack, her perfume wafting into her nose. "They're not going to. I'm one of the hottest girls in school. Plus," Beth took another step closer, her body dangerously close to Mack's. "Even if they did, I don't care. I want to go with you, Mack."

Mack's heart fluttered, stomach twisting in a pleasant way as Beth's words registered. Beth wanted to go with her. *Her.* Mack.

To be her date and they could get to the secret girlfriend stuff later.

"I—thank you," Mack said, shoving her hands deep into her pockets to resist the urge to reach out and touch Beth. Big hazel eyes looked up at her and Mack found it extremely difficult not to lean down and kiss her. Something over Beth's shoulder caught Mack's eye and she looked up to see Meghan walking quickly towards them. She frowned in confusion before a realization hit her.

"Shit."

Meghan pinched Mack hard on the arm and she flinched.

"Ow! What was that for?" Mack asked, rubbing the spot.

Meghan stared at Mack for a moment, clearly unamused, before she held up a familiar tube. Dr. Pepper Lip Smackers.

Shit.

"You left this at my house the other night," Meghan said with an angry look.

Beth frowned and tugged lightly on the edge of Mack's shirt to get her attention. "Why were you at her house?"

Mack only chanced a small look at Beth before shaking her head. She looked between them for a moment before settling on Meghan.

"It's just Chapstick."

Meghan stomped her foot. "It's Dr. Pepper Lip Smackers! Only one person actually likes that flavor!" Meghan's eyes were practically blazing with anger. "I knew you tasted like repressed childhood."

She held the tube out to Beth with a stiff smile. Beth looked at it and Meghan just shook it in front of her face.

"I believe this is yours."

Beth finally took it, staring at it like it would explain to her what was going on at this moment. Mack's heart felt like a hummingbird in her chest as she prayed to whatever god was listening that Meghan would leave it at this and walk away.

Instead Meghan shoved her shoulder. "You said I was the only one you were hooking up with. Now the whole plan is ruined. I'm trying to get the gay out but it doesn't work if you keep replenishing the gay with Beth."

Mack's mouth opened and closed like a fish, throat closing. She was at a loss for words and Beth's hurt face looking up at her certainly didn't help.

"You...kissed her too?" Beth asked quietly. "I thought you weren't kissing the other cheerleaders. You said I was the only one you wanted to kiss."

"Technically, I didn't lie," Mack tried.

She couldn't help the guilty look that passed over her face as she looked down at Beth and shook her head. Hazel eyes filled with tears and Mack reached for her hand. Beth pulled away and Mack was sure she could feel her heart crack. Meghan was staring at her, furious and looking for an explanation, while Beth looked like Mack just kicked her puppy. This situation literally couldn't get any worse.

Except it did.

Daphne materialized and stood next to Meghan. She didn't notice the tension among the three and just looked at Mack.

"Are you coming over and polishing my wood for me tonight?"

All the color drained from Mack's face. "Uh."

"Daphne too?" Beth whispered.

Mack immediately looked down at her and shook her head. "No. Beth, it's not—we didn't—"

"You're giving me *twice* the gay back?" Meghan practically yelled in disbelief.

Mack stood frozen for a moment, unsure of what to do. Meghan looked like she was going to kill her. She slowly backed up, deciding escape was the best option here. Without another word, she turned and began to power walk away, ignoring Meghan and Daphne's yelling after her. She chanced a look over her shoulders and saw the two of them running after her. Mack began to run faster and pat her pockets.

"Shit, shit, shit, where the fuck are my keys?" she said under her breath. Daphne and Meghan had almost caught up to her so Mack took off in a run down the hall. "I can't believe I'm breaking the rules."

She broke into a full sprint, leaving the hall and bursting into the parking lot. She didn't look where she was going and started across the lot, only to have a car honk at her and stop just before hitting her.

Veronica poked her head out of the car. "What the hell, freak? I almost hit you!"

Mack looked back over her shoulder to see Daphne and Meghan pointing at her, closing in on her. She panicked and ran to the passenger side of Veronica's car, opening the door and throwing herself inside.

"Drive!"

"What the hell?"

"Just drive! Please!"

Veronica rolled her eyes as Mack scooted low in her seat. "Fine!"

Mack watched in the right-side mirror as Meghan and Daphne got smaller and smaller, the car pulling away from them. She breathed a sigh of relief and looked over at Veronica.

"This could be considered kidnapping, you know," Veronica said as they pulled out of the school. Mack ignored her and just let herself breathe for a moment. She was in Veronica's car. She had just gotten chased by two crazy cheerleaders, broken another's heart, but she was in *Veronica's car*. Many a daydream had involved being in this car, usually ending with them in the backseat and other embarrassing scenarios. Mack flushed as she remembered and cleared her throat.

"Are you hungry?" Mack asked with the most charming smile she could muster.

Veronica shifted. "No."

"Don't lie," Mack said knowingly. "I see what you cheerleaders use as excuses for meals."

"Fine, maybe a little," Veronica said.

"Then let's go get food," Mack said, much more confident on the outside when internally she was having a panic attack from being in the car of the girl she'd had a crush on for years.

"With you? What are we going to do? Go to a gay bar?"

"No," Mack said, rolling her eyes. "I eat normal food, you know."

Veronica tapped her fingers on the steering wheel and Mack tried not to stare. She was just so damn pretty. She thought about all the times she thought of holding her hand and kissing her cheek. Hell, even just talking to her.

"Fine," Veronica finally said, "but we have to go somewhere away from school so we won't run into anyone we know. Well, anyone *I* know. I doubt you know that many people besides your immediate family."

Mack smiled dumbly. "I knew you'd agree."

Veronica muttered. "Fine. Just don't think this is one of your little dates."

Mack tried to lessen her smile as she put on her seatbelt but ended up grinning like an idiot out of the window.

CHAPTER NINE

Mack chewed on her sandwich slowly, the soggy bread nearly falling apart in her hands. She didn't know why she decided to have Veronica go to the cheapest and clearly grossest sandwich shop in town. Though in her defense, she panicked at the last second when the cheerleader asked Mack what she wanted to eat. It was a question she hadn't been expecting.

Veronica didn't seem to mind though. She'd gotten a salad, which Mack should have known would be the case no matter where they went. After getting the food, Veronica insisted they go eat them at a lookout close by, for fear that someone from school might see them together. Mack was in no position to argue. It was a miracle she was even here with Veronica to begin with. Maybe jumping in front of a moving car *did* have its perks.

Still, she sat in silence. Veronica had given her strict instructions not to engage with her. But Mack felt her fingers twitching. Throwing her extra pieces of bread to the pigeons clearly wasn't enough to keep her occupied anymore. Especially since she kept thinking about Beth and how hurt she looked.

"Can I talk now?" she blurted, cringing a little when the back rivet of her jeans scraped against the hood of Veronica's car that they were sitting on.

Veronica frowned. "Fine. If you must."

She stabbed at her salad a little aggressively and Mack flinched. She never thought she'd ever have the chance to have Veronica all to herself. Not in a million years. She had dreamed about it, sure, but it could never be reality. Mack fiddled with the last third of her sandwich and just stared at Veronica—at the soft curve of her nose and high cheekbones. Suddenly blue eyes turned on her and Mack froze.

"Well?"

"What?"

Veronica rolled her eyes. "You asked if you could talk. Are you just going to stare all day?"

"Oh! No." Mack looked out toward the horizon and cleared her throat. "Why are you a cheerleader?"

Veronica looked at her, just blinking before stabbing her salad even more aggressively. "I mean, what other choice do I have?"

"You have plenty of choices."

"I don't know what you're talking about."

"You're super smart," Mack said matter-of-factly. "Seriously. You're the smartest person I know."

"It's not enough. I need cheerleading for college," Veronica said.

Mack shook her head. "I don't think that's true."

"But—"

"You're telling me you don't have the highest G.P.A. in our class?" Mack asked with a raised eyebrow. Veronica looked at her for another moment before turning back toward her salad. "Exactly," Mack said.

"Well don't you think you're so smart, that you have me figured out," Veronica mocked. "You don't know me."

"I know enough."

"You don't know shit," Veronica insisted. "I have to get into school on a cheer scholarship. Or else what's the point?"

"You're telling me you want to cheer the rest of your life?"

"Of course not," Veronica said with a small laugh. "But I have to go to Louisville and get good grades and meet my husband. Just like my dad says. It's my only way out of this dumb town."

"So you're getting out of this town just to be a wife to some douchebag who doesn't appreciate you?" Mack asked with an amused chuckle. "Sounds like the dream."

"Oh yeah? And what's your plan?" Veronica said, voice defensive. "What are you going to do after school?"

Mack shrugged and crushed the rest of her sandwich into a ball as she crumpled up the paper. "Hopefully go to a college where I don't get humiliated just because of who I like."

They sat in silence for a moment and Mack felt Veronica physically deflate next to her.

"That must suck," Veronica said softly.

"You have no idea," Mack said with a humorless chuckle.

Veronica sighed. "I'm sorry Chad is such a jerk. And Suzan. And...everyone else." Mack could feel Veronica struggling to continue before she basically choked out. "And...me too."

Mack wanted to throw her arms up in the air in celebration but just shook her head. "It's fine. You're a product of your upbringing. At least that's what my parents keep saying every time I'm made fun of."

"That doesn't make it any better."

"It's as good as it can be. In my situation."

"To be fair, Suzan is a bitch to everyone," Veronica said, rolling her eyes. "She's been trying every stupid trick in the book to get my captain spot for at least a year."

Silence fell over them again and Veronica scooted a little closer to Mack. Their shoulders touched and Mack felt her whole body flush as she looked up at her.

"Can I tell you a secret?" Veronica whispered.

Mack felt her mind going a million miles a minute and she swallowed thickly. Maybe this was it. Maybe this was the time that Veronica admitted to being in love with her too. She held her breath. "Of course."

Veronica licked her lips and pulled her knees to her chest. "I applied to Harvard. Without telling my parents."

Mack felt her body deflate a little in disappointment but she smiled anyway. "That's great!"

Veronica shrugged. "I mean, it's a long shot that I'll get in. But I did it on a whim, and you miss one hundred percent of the shots you don't take, right?"

"Harvard would be lucky to have you," Mack said with a smile. They looked at each other for a moment, Mack's breathing getting shallow before Veronica's phone rang.

"Oh, shit," she said pulling it from her pocket and putting it to her ear. "Hello? Mom, I—…okay. Yes. Yes. Yes ma'am."

Veronica hung up the phone and slipped it back into her pocket with an eye roll.

"Parents?" Mack asked, trying to get rid of some of the tension in her shoulders from the moment before the phone rang.

"Yeah," Veronica said with a sigh. "I have to go."

She slipped off the hood and Mack followed suit, standing awkwardly off to the side while Veronica got in her car.

"Do you need a ride home?" Veronica asked after she rolled down the window.

Mack picked up her backpack from the side of the car and shook her head, rubbing the back of her neck nervously. She wanted to say yes, but she'd rather leave on a high note with Veronica and the more time she spent with her, the more chances there were to mess something up.

"Um…naw. I'm good," Mack said with a weird little salute. "I'll walk."

"Okay. Weirdo," Veronica said with a small affectionate smile before she pulled away. Mack watched Veronica drive away for a moment, but not like in a creepy way. Just in a normal way. *Right?* Right.

She walked up the path back toward the main street. As soon as she went to cross the street she jumped back, a car speeding and coming to a stop in front of her.

"Jesus!" she yelled, hand clutching her chest as her mind caught up with the situation. Mack frowned as the car window rolled down. "Suzan?"

"Hey, homo," she said with a small sneer, looking Mack up and down. "I have some news for you."

Mack shook her head and flipped Suzan off as she started walking away. Suzan's car began to roll next to her and Mack tried to walk a little faster.

"Hey, I'm trying to talk to you. Do I need to speak some kind of gay language?" Suzan asked, lips smacking as she chewed her gum loudly. "Canadian?"

"You know there's no such thing, right?" Mack said, finally looking over at her.

Suzan smiled. "Good. You're talking to me. I have information about your girl, Veronica."

Mack faltered, embarrassed that she was even considering asking her for more information.

"I don't care," she sing-songed.

"I think you do."

"I don't."

"Even if I have information that she's not completely straight?" Suzan said. Mack could practically hear the smirk in her voice. It felt like an invasion of privacy. Like if Veronica wanted her to know she would have told her. Not to mention the fact that Suzan was probably lying…right?

As soon as Mack looked over at Suzan, she let the car roll a little faster. Mack started to jog to keep up and rolled her eyes again.

"Can I like...get in?" Mack panted as she jogged.

Suzan shivered, "Ew, no, I just got it cleaned."

Mack groaned. "You can't just go around outing people, you know! It's not cool."

"Listen, I just want this whole thing figured out before the whole town is infected with your gay," Suzan called airily, with a wave of her hand. "It's like you're a mushroom throwing your gay spores everywhere. It's disgusting."

"What am I supposed to do?"

"Just ask her out, damn it. She likes you."

With that, Suzan put the foot on the gas and sped away. Mack coughed as fumes and dust were kicked up in her face, stopping and putting her hands on her knees to rest. She ran a hand over her face and stood back up, hands on her hips as her mind churned.

Veronica...was gay? At least according to her best friend. And *liked* her? Stranger things had happened, like her being able to make out with even one girl. Maybe she did have a chance. All the way home Mack let her mind review every moment she and Veronica had together and re-examine it through a gay lens.

As soon as she got home, she ran up the stairs but her mother's voice in the kitchen stopped her.

"Mackenzie! Come here for a second."

Mack sighed and headed toward the kitchen as she adjusted the backpack on her shoulder. Her mom was standing at the stove, stirring something in a large pot that smelled like spaghetti. Mack leaned on the counter next to her, to confirm her suspicion.

"Why are you home so late?" she asked casually, but Mack knew it was anything but casual.

"Just hanging out," Mack tried.

Her mom couldn't hide her smile. "With one of your little girlfriends?"

"No, Mom," but she felt her blush increase. "I don't have a— There is no girlfriend. Let alone multiple ones."

"Speaking of, Lila came by earlier—"

"How is that a 'speaking of' moment, Mom?" Mack sputtered, lifting herself up to sit on the edge of the counter.

Her mom shrugged and continued stirring. "I just kind of always thought you and Lila might make a cute couple."

Mack couldn't help the laugh that burst from her mouth at that comment. She hunched over, hand on her stomach as she laughed until her mom hit her with a kitchen rag.

"Mackenzie, stop it," her mother said, stirring a little more vigorously. "You have to admit, you two have gotten very close through the years."

"Mom," Mack tried to reason as her giggles subsided. "Don't you think I would have made a move by now if I had a thing for her?"

"I don't know. You've always been a late bloomer." She tilted her head like she was thinking. "I mean, it seems like we just bought you your first bra."

"Hey," Mack said, cupping her boobs defensively. She looked down at them, two slight road bumps in her shirt. They weren't much, but they would do.

"I'm just saying, I wouldn't be surprised if you two ever got together," her mom said with some finality to it.

Mack opened her mouth to respond but found the breath deflating from her lungs. She had never really thought about it, but Lila *was* her best friend. They did everything together and she couldn't imagine her life without her. That's what love was, right? But she didn't have *romantic* love for Lila. She was just a friend. A best friend.

She shook her head, hands under her thighs as she kicked her legs slightly. "Why would you even think that?"

Her mom shrugged. "You two spend so much time together. And you're always painting each other's nails and cuddling."

"Doing each other's nails isn't gay, first of all," Mack pointed out, looking down at the chipped black paint currently on hers. "But...the cuddling might be a little gay."

Mack didn't look at her mom, knowing the look she was going to see was that knowing look that moms always got when it was implied they were right. She thought of her fight with Lila earlier and cringed, but the thought quickly vanished when she remembered Veronica. Veronica who...liked her?

"Gotta go, Mom," Mack said, suddenly leaping off the sink and heading up to her room.

"What? Are you calling Lila?"

"No!" Mack yelled back before closing her bedroom door behind her.

"Dinner will be ready in a half hour!"

Mack threw herself on her bed, reaching over the side to grab her laptop. She typed into the search bar: *How to tell if a girl is gay.*

The cursor blinked at her for a moment as her finger hovered over the enter key. She quickly hit the delete button and retyped: *How to tell if a girl likes you.*

* * *

How to ask a girl to prom

Mack looked down at her phone, typing into the search bar and scrolling through a few articles—all way too hetero for her liking. But they all seemed far too elaborate anyway.

The overwhelming feeling of guilt still gnawed at her gut. Every time she imagined her and Veronica together at prom, another image of Beth would come to the forefront. Beth sad and heartbroken looking. Technically Beth had asked her to prom and even though Mack hadn't given her a clear answer, she still felt awful for even considering going with Veronica.

Mack had texted Beth a few times the night before but she never answered, even when Mack sent her videos of puppies and kittens being friends and those were her favorites. Mack had resigned herself to the fact that Beth was over her. It was probably for the best anyway. Like Mack had tried to tell Beth, she was better off without her. Beth was pretty and popular but the rest of the school would not hesitate to rip her apart if they got wind that she and Mack were together. Veronica was so popular that she could probably kill someone and still be universally adored. Beth didn't have those same protections.

Even though the thought of Beth being mad at her made Mack's throat close, she tried to forget those feelings by thinking about what Suzan had told her. She had fallen into an internet spiral the night before that included stalking Veronica's social media a little bit. But everything Suzan had said was starting to get to her. When she overanalyzed everything Veronica did, it did kinda seem like she had a thing for Mack or at the very least was queer.

Mack finally looked up from her phone when she ran into someone in the hall. Her heart skipped a beat when she saw Beth in front of her, hazel eyes wide and hands gripping the straps of her backpack so tightly her knuckles looked white. Mack couldn't help but smile, but the serious look on Beth's face squashed down any joy she got from seeing her.

"H-hey," Mack said. "Listen, Beth—"

Beth held up her finger to interrupt Mack, face still serious. "I just wanted to ask you a question."

Mack just gave a small nod in agreement, curiosity winning out even if she just wanted to hug Beth and tell her she was sorry.

"I was just wondering if…all of it's true," Beth said.

"If what's true?"

"If you've been…kissing all the cheerleaders? Like people have been saying." Beth asked softly.

Mack sighed and looked down at her boots, shame burning the back of her neck and tips of her ears. "Yeah. I mean, not *all* the cheerleaders. Just you and one other."

"Meghan?"

"I'm not at liberty to say."

"I saw her yell at you, Mack."

"Then you can make your own judgments."

"So you lied to me," Beth said, voice breaking.

"Technically no," Mack pointed out. "I said you were the only girl I *wanted* to kiss. Not that you were the only one I was kissing."

Beth shook her head, tears visibly welling in her eyes. "You tried to trick me."

"Beth—"

"Just like everyone else," Beth sniffled. "Everyone is always calling me stupid and they think they can lie to me but they can't."

"I don't think you're stupid," Mack said, reaching for Beth but she took a step back.

"You do or you wouldn't have lied to me about Meghan."

"Yeah, but it was whatever," Mack said, finally fed up, mostly with her own idiocy. "It didn't mean anything. None of the cheerleaders meant anything."

"N-none of them?" Beth asked, her voice barely above a whisper.

"No, it was all part of the stupid plan," Mack said as she swung her backpack onto her shoulder. "None of it meant anything."

"Oh, okay," Beth said, her voice shaky. "I'm just going to go."

Beth walked away, her shoulders hunched, head hung low, and Mack realized she was crying. Regret flooded her instantly and she cursed under her breath.

"Shit," she whispered as she took off after Beth. "Wait!"

Beth turned the corner into the main hall and Mack followed right behind, but as soon as they did, Suzan was standing there with her arms crossed.

Mack felt her heart jolt in surprise and she put her hand on her chest to calm it.

"Jesus! Where'd you come from?"

"What's your plan?" Suzan prodded.

Mack rolled her eyes. "What are you talking about? Move, I have to talk to Beth."

A slow, almost evil smile curled Suzan's lips up like a cat with a secret and Mack wondered if she should run. "Veronica broke up with Chad last night. Something about him not supporting her and her discovering new things about herself."

Mack nearly choked on air, thoughts of Beth fading. Veronica broke up with Chad and was *discovering new things about herself.* That was one of the gayest things she had ever heard! And all after hanging out with Mack yesterday. Her mind started to turn, pulling out moments from their past like the time Veronica lent her a pencil. Maybe she *did* have a chance.

"I see that look on your face," Suzan said with a smirk. "Don't ruin your chance, homo."

With that she sauntered away and Mack was left standing in the hallway. The bell rang and she jumped back into action, rushing to her first class of the day.

The first three periods of the day dragged. Mack had texted Beth what felt like a thousand times and went to all the places she knew she liked to hide when she talked to her pet psychic, but Beth wasn't anywhere. Mack was worried about her but hoped she'd just gone home after the whole fiasco.

Mack found herself nervously looking at the clock every few seconds. She was going to ask Veronica to prom. She had decided officially because Beth clearly was ignoring her and *damn* if it didn't seem like Veronica might actually return her crush. Mack had been dubious at first. She wasn't completely convinced that Suzan wasn't just being an asshole, but there was really no reason for Suzan to lie to her about this, right? After all, Suzan was one of the most homophobic people she knew, and the less gay activity she saw, the better. So if she was encouraging it, it had to be true.

After all, Mack *had* been making out with the cheerleaders. Maybe that's what Veronica needed to finally realize what she was missing—that and the time they had spent together yesterday. You couldn't eat sandwiches with someone on top of a car and not develop some kind of bond.

Mack had a plan. She had read all the internet articles about how to ask someone to prom and they were all stupid. But Mack knew she had to be presentable at least. So as soon as the lunch bell rang, she rushed to the drama room and borrowed one of the ties to pair with her button-up shirt. It had a weird stain on the back but Mack chose not to acknowledge it.

In the bathroom, she looked up a video on how to tie a tie and ran a shaky hand through her hair. She straightened her shirt and adjusted the tie one last time before ducking into the nurse's office and taking the flowers out of a vase on the desk when the nurse wasn't looking. As she walked to the lunch room, she shook out the water at the end of the stems. They were a little wilted and sad, but they were the best she could do at the moment.

This would be perfect. Just lovely and understated. Just like Veronica.

When she pushed open the door of the cafeteria, it felt like everyone was staring at her even when she knew they weren't. Everyone was wrapped up in their own little worlds, minding their own business. Lila was sitting at their usual table alone, picking at her lunch tray and Beth was sitting at the end of the cheerleader table, shoulders hunched over as she pushed the food around on her plate. But all Mack could see was Veronica sitting at her usual spot at the cheerleaders table.

Her eyes caught Suzan next to her who was smiling and gave her a small thumbs up. Mack's stomach turned nervously and she let out a shaky breath. She just hoped that people couldn't see how her hands were trembling and felt like they were dripping with sweat.

Mack started what felt like the long walk to the cheerleader table where Veronica sat, talking to whoever was across from her. She smiled and laughed and Mack couldn't help the way her heart tripped over herself at the sight. She licked her lips and let out another soft breath as she stopped next to Veronica, who still hadn't noticed her.

Mack tentatively reached out and tapped her shoulder. She looked up at her, confusion written on her face for a moment as her eyes darted to Mack's tie and flowers.

"H-hey," Mack said nervously. They blinked at each other for a moment before Mack found her voice again. "I um… wanted to know if…you wanted to go to prom with me?"

The hopeful tilt in Mack's voice shook as Veronica stared at her. Mack remembered the flowers in her hand, each second of silence feeling like a million years. Suddenly Mack needed to be rid of the flowers and this situation as her stomach slowly dropped. She pushed the flowers toward Veronica and she took them gingerly. Veronica's jaw worked but no sound was coming out and Mack wished the floor would open up and swallow her. She'd rather be in hell than here even a second longer.

"Mack," she started softly, "I—"

"Did you just ask my girlfriend to prom right in front of me, freak?" Chad's booming voice rang out. Mack turned and for the first time noticed Chad sitting across from Veronica. The blood drained from her face and Chad angrily took a bite out of a chicken nugget. So angrily, actually, that Mack was pretty sure it was some kind of threat.

"I thought—" Mack cut herself off and looked over at Suzan who had the biggest grin on her face. Suddenly she stood up, pointing at Mack and yelling so that the whole school could hear.

"The lezzie just tried to get into Veronica's pants!" she yelled. Everyone in the cafeteria turned to look at them and Mack felt panic rising like bile in her throat.

Veronica grabbed the edge of Suzan's cheerleading top and tugged at her to sit back down. "Stop," she hissed.

Suzan continued on. "Probably because Veronica and Mack were lezzing out together yesterday!"

People started whispering and if Mack had any blood left in her face before she was sure it was all but gone now. She felt sick. Her eyes darted around the cafeteria and she noticed Beth who wasn't even looking at her and Lila with an unreadable expression.

"I'm sorry," Mack whispered to Veronica as she backed away from the table. Veronica looked up at her helplessly, frozen in her seat. Suddenly she felt something hit her on the side of the face and frowned.

She looked down at her feet where a half-eaten chicken nugget sat on the dirty linoleum floor. Chad was laughing behind his hand, and she shook her head. "Did you just throw a chicken nugget at me?"

"Dyke," Chad growled, throwing another nugget at Mack. It went wide and anger flared next to the embarrassment.

"So much for that football scholarship, huh? Can't even throw a goddamn chicken nugget!"

Chad's face turned about five different shades of red before he stood up, grabbed a handful of his mac and cheese and threw it right at Mack's face.

"Get her! Get the dyke!"

Soon, food was flying at Mack from every direction and hitting her. She curled in on herself for a moment before running back toward the cafeteria doors blindly, just managing to stay upright as she slid through the food. She felt the hot prick of tears in the corners of her eyes as she went. Finally she pushed through the doors of the cafeteria and into the nearly silent hall. She stood there for a moment, the laughing in the cafeteria just barely muffled by the cheap school doors. Her hands shook and tears clouded her vision.

"Fuck," she whispered. Her clothes were practically dripping with mac and cheese and whatever other sludge the cafeteria had decided to serve that day. Her heart was beating so hard she was surprised it hadn't burst from her chest and her stomach squeezed too tightly. This was it. This was her worst nightmare.

She quickly wiped some stray tears off of her cheeks as her stunned legs carried her to her car.

She was living her worst nightmare, and she had only done it to herself.

CHAPTER TEN

Mack called out sick the next day at school. She had spent the whole morning texting Beth how she was sorry and didn't mean what she'd said, but at most she got the little bubble that alerted her Beth was typing, then nothing.

After a couple hours of unanswered texts, Mack tried to message Veronica, except she didn't have her number so she just bombarded her on all forms of social media that she could without seeming like a creeper.

And Lila. Mack was sure Lila didn't want to talk to her at all, which was just fine with her. If Lila thought Mack was being ridiculous even after this whole mess was *her* idea…then fine. She could go be the cheerleaders' hand servant if it made her happy. Mack didn't care either way.

Around dinner time, Mack finally made it downstairs. She dragged her feet into the kitchen and slumped down at the table as her mom slid a plate in front of her.

"Mackerel," her dad said as he sat down across from her. "What's wrong?"

"She had a fight with Lila," her mom said.

Mack just groaned as her dad hummed. "Lover's quarrel."

"It's not!" Mack lifted her head from the table with a frown. "Why do you two think Lila and I are together?"

Her dad shrugged and looked at her mom who just busied herself with her own plate. "I guess I just assumed."

"Well, please stop. My love life is complicated enough as it is," Mack said, stabbing at a green bean with her fork.

Her parents looked at each other like they could read each other's minds before looking back at Mack. Her mom sighed and shook her head. "I just think you need to fix things with Lila. You've known each other for so long—"

"I know, Mom," Mack sighed. "We'll see. She kinda hates my guts right now."

"I'm sure she doesn't *hate* you," her dad said.

"Well, she went and joined the cheerleading cleanup team just to get back at me. So, I'd say she's pretty pissed." Mack shoved a green bean into her mouth. "She's not answering any of my texts so I'm going to try and corner her at school tomorrow."

Her parents nodded slowly, looking from Mack to each other once more. Mack felt a twinge of annoyance and rolled her eyes, shoveling more green beans into her mouth.

"And we're not together," Mack said again, hoping she made a point this time. Her dad just held his hands up in surrender and her mom shrugged. Maybe someday she would convince them. Like when she got a real girlfriend. If that day ever came.

* * *

The next day at school was probably one of the worst days of her life. It seemed all perfectly dramatic, but it was true. In the morning she had tried to talk to Lila, but as soon as she saw Mack walking toward her, she took off.

For some reason, people were bullying her more now than they had been when everyone first found out she was gay. She was shoved from behind and had a bruise on her arm where she had been pushed into a locker. Her ears burned in embarrassment as she tried to get her bearings and continue on her way down the hall as if nothing had happened. It felt like she was on the verge of tears all day.

Beth wasn't even at school so Mack's mind went insane thinking of all the reasons she could be out. The thing she kept coming back to was that Beth was so mad at her she couldn't even come to school. She knew it was self-centered, but that's where her mind went.

But Lila ignoring her killed her the most. Lila had been there for her, her rock since the first day of school. Now it felt like she was floundering without her.

Lunch was probably the worst, though, to be fair, Mack brought it on herself. She went through the lunch line with her head down. Mack tried not to think about it too hard. She was going to sit in her usual spot and hope Lila would at least *acknowledge* her, but when she turned away from the counter she saw Veronica standing there at the condiments counter just a foot away.

Mack fidgeted with her tray and took a couple of steps closer, easing her tray next to Veronica's.

"Hey," she said softly, stomach twisting. "I'm…sorry."

Veronica kept staring at the ketchup squeeze out as she pushed the pump so Mack continued.

"I um…Suzan told me you…" Mack felt her face heat. "…that you maybe had a thing for me and you broke up with Chad and I was stupid to believe her."

"Yeah, you were," Veronica said simply. She hit the ketchup pump a little too vigorously. "So please. Stop talking to me."

Veronica turned on her heels and stalked back to her table. Mack blinked at her back, a heavy pressure behind her eyes as she cleared her throat.

After that, she didn't even bother trying to sit in the cafeteria. She just took her tray and sat on the bleachers. The only other kid there was Stuart from band who was too weird to even sit with the other band kids. He spent the whole lunch staring at Mack from the other side of the bleachers with his bologna sandwich.

"Where's your girlfriend?" he asked, voice nasally.

Mack blinked at him. "Which one?" she asked bitterly.

"The scary one," he said, "Lila."

"Why does everyone think she's my girlfriend?" Mack asked herself. She ran a hand through her hair and shook her head. "She's not my girlfriend."

Stuart took a big bite of his sandwich, chewing with his mouth open. "Seems like it. You two seemed pretty chummy. You were always touching her."

Mack forced a laugh despite the heat rising in her face. "No, I wasn't. Not more than a normal friend."

"I don't touch my friends like that."

"Shut up, Stuart," Mack mumbled as she stood up from the bleachers, her tray held tightly in her hands. "You don't know anything about female friendship." Mack left it at that as she stomped down the bleachers, throwing her entire tray in the trash can.

Okay.

So maybe Lila was Mack's best friend who knew every little thing about her, the person who loved her and she loved back. The person she would do *anything* for. The one that made it feel like she was missing a limb whenever she wasn't around. It didn't mean she was *in* love with her...right?

Mack stopped in front of her locker and looked at the picture of her and Lila taped on the inside, the one where their faces were pressed together, cheek to cheek, and their smiles took over their entire faces.

"Well...shit," Mack said to herself as she shut her locker.

Mack came up with the best worst idea ever. Literally ever. It would determine everything. It would tell her whether or not she was in love with Lila as more than a friend.

It could also cement Lila's hate for her, but well, Mack had nothing else to lose at this point. She had spent the last three hours of school analyzing every single interaction she'd had with Lila in the last year or so. And she was starting to question her feelings for her best friend along with everyone else.

She had determined that if this was a stupid teen movie, she would be in love with Lila. So there was only one way to figure out if she had feelings for her or not.

That's how Mack ended up standing in front of Lila's house. She had her hands stuffed in the pockets of her jacket, rocking back and forth on her heels. Was this a bad idea? Probably. But still not as bad as trying to steal all the cheerleaders from their boyfriends.

"All right," Mack said, trying to psyche herself out by shaking out her limbs. "I want to figure this out once and for all. Maybe I'm in love with my best friend. We'll see."

Her fist hovered over the door for a moment before she took a deep breath and knocked three times quickly. There was the sound of someone coming down the stairs before the door opened. Mack's heart already felt lighter when she saw Lila standing there in basketball shorts and a hoodie. But as soon as Lila saw her, she shut the door with a roll of her eyes.

Mack frowned and knocked again. "Lila! Open up!"

"I'm not home!" Lila called from the other side of the door.

Mack rolled her eyes and leaned her forehead against the door with a dull thump. "Lila, please? I'm really sorry. I'm sorry I was such an asshole and I'm sorry I drove you to join the shitty part of the cheerleading team. I know you don't even get a cute uniform."

There was silence for a moment and Lila opened up the door just a crack and Mack stumbled forward before straightening up. Just big enough for her to barely see through.

"You were a huge asshole," Lila said.

"I know," Mack breathed, relieved that Lila was even talking to her. "I know I was and I'm so so sorry. I shouldn't have ignored you. You're…You're my ride or die bitch."

"Your emotional bra?" Lila asked softly.

Mack chuckled and smiled warmly. "Yeah. My emotional bra."

Lila opened the door a little wider, shoving her body in the space between the door and the frame as she looked at Mack. She fiddled with the loose strings in her pockets to avoid reaching for Lila, even though her body was itching to.

Mack licked her lips and shrugged. "I'm sorry."

"I'm sorry too," Lila mumbled. "I was a bit dramatic about the whole thing. I was just—" Lila pulled on the strings on the front of her sweatshirt and sighed. "I was jealous. You were getting all this attention from other girls and you didn't have time for me anymore and…it hurt. I know I need to let you spread your gay wings and fly but I don't know. And then I thought by joining the team you'd pay more attention to me again."

Mack felt her heart beat a little faster. Was this it? Was this "the moment" that every stupid high school movie had?

"Well, you would look really cute in that uniform," Mack confessed with an awkward smile.

Lila tilted her head, light eyes on Mack for the first time since she got there. "You think so?"

Mack rubbed the back of her neck and shifted nervously. "Yeah."

"Mack…have you ever…?"

Suddenly her mouth felt dry. "Have I ever…what?"

Lila didn't say anything else. She just put her hands on either side of Mack's face, took a step forward and kissed her square on the mouth. Mack's mind reeled in surprise for a moment at the feeling of Lila's lips against hers, stomach squeezing a little.

Lila pulled back and blinked at Mack. "Did you feel anything?"

Mack's mouth opened and closed like a fish. "I mean…Your lips are a little chapped—"

"No, focus," Lila said, squishing Mack's face a little. "Did you feel *anything?*"

Mack licked her lips. Kissing Lila was…nice. But it was just like kissing the other cheerleaders. Nice and definitely fun. Mack obviously didn't have a whole lot of experience in this department, but all of the books and fanfiction she had read always talked about the first kiss like it was the most dramatic thing in the world. Like when their lips met, there should be full thunderstorms up and down her spine or flowers should spontaneously bloom around them. *Something.* Maybe she was doing it wrong. Or maybe she had been oversold on this whole kissing thing. She didn't have the fluttery heartbeat or the stomach ache inducing joy that happened when she kissed…

Oh.

Mack looked at Lila carefully. If she really thought about the facts, she should be into Lila. They'd been best friends forever, clearly compatible. Mack thought she was super hot, even if it was in an objective kind of way. But kissing Lila wasn't like—

Well it wasn't like kissing Beth.

Mack just blinked at Lila and her shoulders fell.

"Me either," Lila sighed, sounding relieved as she dropped her hands from Mack's face. "I thought maybe we were super stereotypical. The whole being in love with your best friend thing."

Mack smiled, "Yeah, me too."

Still, she couldn't stop thinking about Beth and how her lips were so soft and tasted like Dr. Pepper Lip Smackers. Mack frowned and stuffed her hands in her pockets again. "Can I come in? Are we good?"

Lila smiled and pulled Mack into the house by her arm. "Duh. And now I can quit the stupid cheer squad."

Mack shivered. "I don't know why you did that to yourself."

"I was panicking. It seemed like the right thing to do," Lila confessed as she closed the door. Mack looked around the entryway nervously, unable to stop thinking about Beth. And kissing her. And touching her.

God, she was gay.

"What's wrong with you?" Lila asked as she started up the stairs to her bedroom, Mack following behind.

"Um…" Mack fidgeted. "Is it too soon to talk about the cheerleaders again?"

Lila turned quickly and stared Mack down. "Depends."

"Depends on what?" Mack asked.

Lila didn't say anything until they got to her room. Both of them threw themselves on the bed, the mattress bouncing under them. Mack pulled a pillow to her chest while Lila propped her head up on her elbow to better look at her.

"All right, just tell me and I'll cut you off if you get annoying," Lila said with a skeptical eyebrow raise.

Mack groaned and bit her lip. "Well, I think I have a real-life crush."

"On one of the cheerleaders?" Lila asked. "We already knew that. Stupid Veronica—"

"No…not Veronica," Mack said.

Lila gasped and hit Mack's arm in disbelief. "No way. Who?"

"Beth," Mack confessed, her voice small. Lila's eyes got big and Mack put her pillow over her face. "I can't help it! She's just so cute and sweet and a really good kisser! And we have way more in common than I ever thought we would. Seriously. We play all the same video games and she's also obsessed with those videos of hamsters eating tiny plates of food."

Lila wrestled Mack's pillow from her face to get a better look at her face. "Does she like you too?"

"Probably not anymore," Mack sighed. "I fucked up with her too."

"What'd you do, dumbass?" Lila asked.

Mack grimaced. "I basically told her it didn't matter."

Lila gasped. "Shit."

"I didn't mean it like that!" Mack groaned, covering her face with her hands. "I was just upset and it came out all wrong and I made her cry."

Lila smacked Mack with the pillow and she screamed. "Ow!"

"You fucking idiot!" Lila said. "Beth is like the hottest cheerleader and you fucked it up!"

"I didn't mean to!" Mack insisted, trying to block herself from the barrage of pillow hits from Lila.

"Okay, well now we have to fix it," Lila said holding the assaulting pillow to her stomach. "You have to make it up to her."

"How?" Mack asked, rolling onto her side. "I really messed up. I don't think she'll want to talk to me anymore."

Lila shook her head. "You really know nothing about girls. There's always a way to get them back if you're not a total dick the second time around too. What does she like?"

"Um. Taco Bell, Beanie Babies—"

"Beanie Babies?" Lila said with a raised eyebrow.

Mack sat up defensively. "Yes, it's cute. Don't make fun of her."

Lila held up her hands defensively. "All right. Well, I actually think my mom has all my old Beanie Babies in the garage still."

An idea popped into Mack's head and she sat up straight. "Does your mom still do those fake flower arrangements?"

"Yeah."

"All right. I have a plan," Mack said with a wide smile. "Will you help me?"

Lila tilted her head like she was thinking. "Do you promise not to ignore me again once Beth is back to making out with you?"

"I promise," Mack said holding out her pinky. "With my whole heart."

Lila looked down at the pinky for a moment before linking hers with Mack's and smiling. "Then let's get you the cheerleader."

Mack fidgeted nervously, pulling on the sleeves of her suit jacket and running a hand through her hair. She choked a little when Lila pulled on her tie to get her attention. She was sitting on the hood of Mack's car, Mack in front of her as she tried to tie her tie for her. Lila's phone was open on her lap watching a how-to video.

"Stop moving," Lila mumbled, squinting as she tightened the knot. Mack made an effort not to move as she focused on her breathing. Lila's tongue was sticking out of her mouth in concentration, brow furrowed as she took one final look at Mack. "All right. My work here is done."

Mack adjusted the tie a little and looked down at herself. She and Lila had gone to the mall the night before and bought a suit for Mack. It was simple, black with a white button-down shirt underneath. And yeah, maybe she did get it from the little boys' section but she still looked good. She wanted everything to be perfect for Beth.

"Are you sure about this?" Lila finally asked.

"Nope," Mack said easily.

"And you still want to do it?"

"Yep."

Lila sighed and put a heavy hand on Mack's shoulder. "As your best friend and former love interest—"

"I don't—"

"Ssh," Lila said with a shake of her head. "As your best friend and *former love interest*, it's my duty to remind you what happened last time you asked a cheerleader to prom."

Mack cringed and ruffled her own hair a little. Lila scoffed and batted her hands away as she tried to fix Mack's hair again.

"I'm…repressing that," Mack sighed. "Even if it's the only thing I'll ever be known for in school."

Lila, seemingly satisfied with Mack's hair again, and straightened out her lapels. "Beth is *still* a cheerleader. What if the same thing happens?"

Mack shook her head. "It doesn't matter. She's worth the risk. She's worth…everything. I need her to know that. I will risk getting chicken nuggets and pudding thrown at me every day if it means I get to just apologize to her and tell her how I feel."

"I thought it was mac and cheese," Lila said with a tilt of her head. Mack shot her a look and Lila just smiled widely. "Look at you."

Mack reached for her face. "What? Do I have something on my face?"

"No, dummy," Lila said, pulling Mack's hand away from her face and holding it on her lap. "Look at you! All queer and adorable and going after the girl you like. It's sweet."

Mack shrugged and gave Lila a lopsided smile. "I just really, really like her."

"You're so cute!" Lila exclaimed as she squeezed Mack's cheek.

She hit Lila's hand away. "Stop," Mack mumbled through her smile. She wiggled her eyebrows at Lila as she put her hands in her pockets. "Sure you don't have a crush on me?"

Lila rolled her eyes. "You wish. Now stop pining for me and let's get you your girl."

Mack smiled and nodded. "Okay. You good to get her to the park?"

"I'll kidnap her if I have to," Lila said jumping off the hood and spinning Mack's car keys on her finger. She slid her sunglasses over her eyes and gave Mack the thumbs up. "Don't worry about me. Just have your shit set up for when I get her here."

"Got it," Mack said, watching as Lila got in the car and started it. "Don't actually kidnap her."

Lila purposefully turned up the radio. "What?"

"Don't actually—" Mack sighed as Lila shook her head and started to pull away, still pretending like she couldn't hear her. "I know 'Jawbreaker' is your favorite movie but we don't need a reenactment!"

"Great movie!" Lila agreed as she pulled away, leaving Mack in the middle of the park to wait.

"Will you go to prom with me? Will *you* go to prom with me? Will you go to *prom* with me?" Mack practiced under her breath as she paced in front of her carefully laid out proposal.

Mack looked down at her handiwork. Dozens of packs of Lip Smackers, all spelling out *Prom?* on the grass. She had just laid down the final blister pack when she heard a car approaching. She looked behind her and saw Lila pulling up, Beth sitting in the passenger seat with a blindfold over her eyes.

Her stomach flipped just to see her sitting there. Lila gave her a thumbs up and Mack picked up her handmade bouquet off the ground, if you could call it a bouquet. It was just a bunch of Beanie Babies arranged to look like a bouquet that Mack and Lila had made the night before. She held it behind her back so that Beth couldn't see.

Lila helped Beth out of the car and Mack's heart fluttered. She was in her usual cheer uniform, hands clasped nervously behind her back as Lila carefully walked her toward Mack. Beth was standing in front of Mack when Lila nodded at her and removed the blindfold. Beth blinked and blew her bangs from her eyes as the blindfold fell.

Mack felt her breath catch in her throat when Beth's light eyes finally landed on her and all the words she'd been practicing flew from her mind.

"Hey," she whispered.

Beth smiled nervously, crossing her arms. "Hey," she said before looking down at her feet. "What do you want?"

Mack took a deep breath and ducked her head a little to look in Beth's eyes. "I'm...I want to apologize, first of all." Beth looked up at her and Mack felt a little bit of hope flutter in her chest. "I'm really sorry I was such a jerk. I shouldn't have said those things that I said to you. You didn't mean 'nothing.' Kissing you meant *everything*."

Beth blinked at her. A small smile briefly flitted over her lips before it disappeared. She folded and unfolded her hands in front of her. "Is this because Veronica rejected you?"

"No," Mack said quickly, "not at all. I don't like her that way. I realized that, yeah, I liked kissing all the cheerleaders and it was fun, but the only person I wanted to kiss was you. But when I realized it, it was too late."

Mack's throat was tight with emotion, mouth dry as she tried to get a read on Beth. She saw her eyes shining with tears and got worried that she had fucked up again. Quickly, she pulled the bouquet from behind her back and held it out.

"I made you this."

Beth stared at the bouquet and looked back up at Mack, taking a step closer to her.

"You made this? For me?"

"Yeah. Lila helped."

Beth reached out and took the bouquet, cradling it carefully between her hands. She smiled brightly and Mack felt her heart leap in joy. She couldn't help but smile back as Beth held the bouquet to her chest.

"But...a lot of these are rare," Beth said. "How did you find them?"

Mack shrugged, stuffing her hands in her pockets. "It um, actually wasn't that hard." Mack shook her head. "So…do you forgive me?"

Beth tilted her head like she was thinking and Mack's heart stopped for a moment. But the small, beautiful smile that bloomed on Beth's face started it again.

"I forgive you," Beth said. "I get it. You were like a kid at Disneyland for the first time. Suddenly all these girls wanted you and you couldn't resist."

"But I only want you," Mack reiterated, reaching for Beth, hands on her arms. "So that's why…I wanted to ask you to prom."

Mack stepped aside so that Beth could see 'Prom?' spelled out in the Lip Smackers. Her eyes got wide and she smiled brighter than Mack thought possible.

"Yes," Beth said, clutching the bouquet tighter. She hopped in excitement and giggled. "Yes!"

Mack stumbled when Beth threw her arms around her neck. Her hands automatically found Beth's waist and held her close. She breathed her in for a moment, her head feeling light with Beth's face pressed to her neck. Mack was sure her heart was doing somersaults in her chest.

Relief flooded her and she squeezed Beth a little tighter just as she pulled back. Their faces were close and Mack felt her breath catch in her throat.

"I missed you," Mack blurted. She could feel the tips of her ears heat in a blush.

Beth's fingers played with the hairs at the base of Mack's neck and she shivered, involuntarily, bringing Beth closer.

"I missed you too," Beth said, eyes flickering down to Mack's lips. Without thinking, Mack leaned down and kissed her. Fireworks exploded in Mack's mind and she sighed in relief. Kissing Beth was nothing like kissing anyone else. There was a Beanie Baby bouquet squished between them and Lila was two yards away but it felt good.

It felt *right*.

It was like a slow heat, building between them. Chills erupted over her whole body and she never wanted to stop kissing Beth. Ever. But a loud wolf whistle from Lila, who was leaning against the car, broke them from their moment.

Mack pulled away slowly but kept her face close to Beth's, their foreheads resting together. Both of them had uncontrollable smiles on their faces as they just looked at each other. Mack sighed and kissed Beth briefly again. Maybe things were finally looking up.

CHAPTER ELEVEN

"All right, twirl," Lila commanded from the other side of the computer screen. Mack frowned but did what she asked. She had insisted on video chatting with Mack while they got ready since they wouldn't be driving there together. Rather, Lila told Mack they couldn't drive together because Mack had a girlfriend now and she "wasn't no third wheel."

"The back of your jacket has something on it," Lila said, leaning closer to the screen. Mack tried to turn and get a good look at it as she blindly brushed at it. "It looks like cat hair. How is that possible? You don't even have a cat. Are you just that gay?"

Mack shot Lila a look and turned back to face the computer. "Other than the cat fur, everything look okay?"

Mack was just going to wear the suit she got from the little boy's section again, but when her mom found out that she had a real date to prom, she insisted on taking her to a tailor and getting a real suit and a gold bow tie Beth helped her pick out to match her dress, and she was good to go.

"You look great," Lila confirmed. She winked and added, "Are you trying to make me realize what I'm missing out on? Because it's not working. Have you seen my dress?"

Lila stepped away from the computer to show off her red dress that hugged her curves and accentuated her legs. Mack cleared her throat.

"Yes, I have. Very nice," she mumbled as she adjusted her tie for the fifth time.

"Hey, maybe I'll snag a cheerleader tonight," Lila joked.

"Good luck. I have the best one anyway."

Lila pretended to gag but smiled. "I actually really like Beth."

"I knew you would," Mack said as she made sure her shirt was tucked in.

"I didn't realize she could name all the contestants of 'Top Model' since season one," Lila said, shaking her head and looking impressed. "Like…damn. I might have to steal her from you."

Mack pointed at the screen. "Don't even try."

Lila waved her hand dismissively. "Don't worry. For some reason that girl is head over heels for you. I wouldn't stand a chance."

Mack smiled proudly just as the doorbell rang. "Ah, she's here. I'll see you there, okay?"

"Okay, bitch, see you there. Tell your mom to text me pictures of the two of you. I need a new phone background."

"A phone background of me and my girlfriend?"

"Duh. I'm the biggest Macbeth shipper there is," Lila said. "Okay. Go get your girl. I'll see you later. Love you! Bye!"

"Bye!" Mack said just as Lila hung up. Shutting her computer, Mack took one last look in the mirror before grabbing the corsage off her dresser and heading down the stairs. She took them two at a time, only tripping once before getting to the front door. She took a deep breath and adjusted her suit jacket one more time before opening the door.

The air left her lungs as soon as she laid eyes on Beth. Her hair was up and revealed the long lines of her neck. Her dress was strapless and dipped low in the front, the gold material hugging her tightly and flaring off into a skirt at the bottom.

Mack smiled stupidly. "Wow." Beth blushed and Mack continued. "You're beautiful. I mean. You're always beautiful. Just like…you're extra beautiful and— "

Beth kissed Mack soundly on the lips. She felt herself relax into the kiss with Beth's hands framing her cheeks. The sound of a camera clicking interrupted their moment and they turned to see Mack's mom snapping pictures.

"Mom," Mack complained as she snapped a couple more photos. Beth didn't seem to mind, though. She put her arms around Mack's waist and kissed her cheek so that her mom could snap a few more.

"What? I'm excited for my baby's first date," her mom said as she snapped another picture. "Gordon! Get in here! Beth's here!"

"I'm coming!"

Mack groaned. "I'm sorry."

"It's cute," Beth whispered in her ear. Her hot breath sent a chill down Mack's spine and she turned to putty in Beth's arms. "And you look good. Let her take all the pictures."

Mack remembered the corsage in her hand. "Oh!" She took a step away from Beth and held the flower between them. "Madam."

Beth held out her wrist and Mack's hands shook nervously as she slipped the corsage onto it. She adjusted it so it sat just right on her wrist, Mack's fingers trailing over Beth's palm as she pulled her hand away.

"Perfect," Mack said with a smile.

Beth looked at it, a permanent smile on her face, as she kissed Mack's cheek again. "Thank you."

"All right, you two lovebirds," Mack's mom said, her dad behind her. "Let's get a couple more pictures and then you can get on your way. And Mackerel, don't worry, I already texted Lila the picture she asked for."

Mack sighed. "Don't you think it's kinda weird you text my best friend?"

Her parents looked at each other, clearly confused. "No. Why would it be?" her mom asked. "I thought she was going to be my daughter-in-law there for a bit."

"Mom," Mack chastised.

Beth shrugged. "I kinda thought you two were into each other for a while too. She always stole your chicken nuggets at lunch."

Mack covered her face with her hands. "God, why did everyone think that?"

"You guys touch a lot."

"Okay, well, anyway," Mack said, "can we get this over with so that we can get to the dance?"

"Fine, fine," her mom said. They arranged themselves into the traditional prom poses and Mack went along with it. It was embarrassing as these things usually were with her parents fussing over her. But she had to admit, it was kind of amazing that she was getting this "typical" high school moment since Mack didn't think she'd ever get to experience it. Dressing up and going to prom...sure. But her parents wanting to take a thousand pictures of her and her date as they stood on the stairs and held each other? That was something she never thought would happen.

"Okay, we can be done," her dad said, carefully reaching over and confiscating the camera from her mother's hands. Her mom sighed but nodded, tears shining in her eyes.

"You're both just so beautiful," she sniffled.

Mack took that as her cue to leave. "Thanks, Mom," she said, lacing her fingers with Beth's. "I'll be home by midnight."

"Be safe, girls," her dad said as they walked toward the door. "Hey, Mackerel."

Mack stopped as she stepped out the door and turned to look at him, worried about what embarrassing thing was about to come out of his mouth.

He smiled and put his hand on her shoulder, shaking her a little. "I'm proud of you."

Mack looked surprised for a moment before smiling. "Thanks, Dad."

He winked and handed her a wad of cash. "Just in case. Now get out of here."

"Thank you."

Mack smiled as she put the money in her pocket and led Beth out to her car. She opened the door for her, earning her a small peck on the lips before Beth slid inside. Mack practically skipped over to the driver's side and got in.

The ride to school felt oddly short. Mack let Beth pick the music and they just talked about…well nothing really. But Mack could talk about nothing with Beth forever, as cheesy as it seemed.

It was almost a little disappointing when Mack pulled into the gym parking lot. Her stomach had gotten twisted in knots, and the way Beth was stroking the top of her hand didn't seem to help.

"Are you sure you want to go to prom?" Mack asked, thinking about food flying at her face and the way her peers had laughed at her. "My dad gave me a bunch of cash. We could go somewhere else. Anywhere else."

Beth squeezed Mack's hand. Beth's soft smile helped a little and Mack couldn't help but smile back.

"Mack, we don't have to go if you don't want to, but I really want to go. And I won't let the other kids bother you. I promise."

Mack bit her lip and looked at Beth, wanting to believe her.

"I…They hate me," she mumbled. "I know they're going to give me a hard time and they're going to see you with me and give you a hard time too."

Beth shrugged. "Then we'll deal with it together."

"People are going to think you're gay," Mack said softly.

They'd been careful at school the couple of days between her promposal and the dance. They sat out at the bleachers at lunch and only stole glances at each other in the halls. They certainly didn't go to school the next day holding hands and waving rainbow flags.

The bullying had started to wind down with people more excited and interested in prom than anything else. But this was going to be a kiss of death for Beth.

"Actually, I have something to show you," Beth said opening her clutch and rummaging around until she found the button for the gay alliance she had started. She pinned it to the front of her dress and Mack noticed a few words crossed out: *Friends of LGBTQ (but only friends and definitely not gay) Club.*

It took a moment for her brain to process what it said before she looked back up at Beth. "But— "

"You inspired me," Beth said. "Before all of this I was pretty sure I didn't like boys the same way other girls did, but I never really thought about it because it was too scary and my priest told me it wasn't allowed. I just ignored those feelings and hoped they would go away. Then when I found out you were gay… Well, you'd always been so nice to me and I always thought there was no way that Jesus could send you to hell just because you liked girls. Then when we kissed I knew there was no way I could feel the same way about boys as I did for girls. Well, you, mostly. And you…inspired me."

"I…no. There's nothing here to inspire anyone," Mack said gesturing to herself. "I'm a loser— "

"You're not," Beth insisted. "Think about it. You were outed by a stupid football player and didn't let that get you down. Instead you told them you were going to get back at them and you…well, you *did*. You didn't let them keep you from being yourself and that's really cool."

Mack felt her cheeks burning as she stared down at her hands. "I guess I just never thought about it that way."

Beth's hand on her cheek made her turn her head toward her. "Well, it's true. You're inspiring. Like Kate McKinnon or Captain Marvel." Beth scrunched her nose cutely for a moment before she amended her statement. "Or like…Lizzie Borden."

"The…murderer?" Mack asked with a raise of her eyebrow.

Beth shrugged. "Have you ever read about her? She's super interesting. And probably gay."

Mack chuckled. "You're cute."

She leaned forward to kiss her just as there was a knock on the window. Mack groaned and turned to see Lila waving at them.

"Stop making out and let's go in!" she said. Mack flipped Lila off and leaned over to kiss Beth quickly on the lips before she practically ran to the other side to open the door for her.

Beth looped her arm through Mack's and squeezed gently as all three of them walked toward the gym. The closer they got, the more nervous Mack felt. They had passed a few people on the way and a couple gave them a double take, but each time Beth's hand just squeezed Mack's arm a little tighter.

Mack put her hand over Beth's and ran her thumb over her knuckles. They stopped right before the balloon arch that was over the entrance to the gym. Mack turned to Beth, hand still covering hers.

"It's not too late to go as just friends," Mack said, licking her lips nervously. It would break her heart if Beth decided to keep up the friends charade, but she felt like she owed her the option.

Beth shrugged. "Even if they make fun of us, we only have two months left of school. Then it's college where no one cares. I actually checked and USC has a bunch of queer student groups."

Mack blinked. "You're going to USC?"

Beth waved it off. "They begged me."

"I didn't even know you applied. USC is super hard to get into."

"I know!" Beth smiled proudly. "I think my cheerleading plus all the time I spent volunteering at the vets' offices helped. Now let's go."

Mack and Lila shared a look before Beth laced her fingers with Mack's and pulled her into the gym. It was done up with a stage at the far end, balloons and colored lights everywhere. It wasn't anything special, but it was still amazing. The dance floor was already flooded with students moving to the beat and Mack could feel Beth's excitement radiating off her. It was contagious.

In the dimmed lights of the room, her nerves had started to dissipate. Maybe tonight wouldn't be as bad as she thought.

"Let's dance," Beth said, squeezing Mack's hand and leaning close to her. "Please?"

Mack looked over at Lila who was already shooing them away. "I'm going to find the spiked punch bowl. Have fun and save room for Jesus, you two!"

Mack rolled her eyes just as Beth pulled her out to the middle of the dance floor. Her hands were sweating and her hips moved awkwardly, so Mack just swayed along with Beth.

"See, this is nice," Beth said, fingers raking through the hair at the back of Mack's skull.

"Yeah, it is," Mack admitted, her hands tightening on Beth's waist. The song changed to a slower one and Mack swallowed thickly when Beth stepped closer to her. She glanced around and no one was looking at them. Even the teachers patrolling the dance floor seemed more interested in the straight couples practically humping each other rather than them. Thankfully.

She noticed Veronica dancing nearby with Chad, her forcing him to stay an arm's length away. Veronica looked up, her eyes meeting Mack's, and she smiled awkwardly. Mack smiled back, offering her a small wave before putting her hand back on

Beth's waist. The song ended and Mack reluctantly moved a little further away from Beth.

There was some feedback with the microphone on the stage and everyone cringed. They looked toward the stage and Principal Berkley was standing there sheepishly. He cleared his throat and smiled out at everyone. Lila pushed her way through the crowd and popped up next to Mack.

"Why do they make us suffer through this king and queen bullshit?" she muttered, lifting a cup of juice to her lips. "We know who's gonna win. Chad and fucking Veronica. Boring."

"Hello, students. Now is the portion of the night you've all been waiting for." The principal paused in what Mack supposed was meant to be dramatic. "The announcement of your Prom King and Queen."

Lila gagged and made a jack-off motion with her hand. Mack snickered and bumped her shoulder into Lila's. She offered Mack a sip of her drink and she took it without thinking, sputtering when it just tasted like pure alcohol.

"I see you found the spiked one," Mack said, wiping off her mouth with the back of her hand.

"Girl, I spiked this shit myself," Lila said taking another sip.

"First! For Prom Queen we have…" The principal revealed the envelope with a flourish and opened it. He took a deep breath as he read the card and leaned into the microphone with a wide smile. "Veronica Ryder!"

There was a lot of applause, Mack and Beth included. Lila clapped slowly. "Oh my god, I'm so surprised," she said sarcastically, making Mack laugh again. Veronica went on the stage and got her sash and crown, standing behind the principal with a wide smile.

"And now, for your Prom King…" Principal Berkley pulled out a second envelope. "Your Prom King is…" He squinted for a second, holding the card closer to his face to read it again. He cleared his throat and smiled stiffly. "Your Prom King is… Mackenzie Gomez."

Mack felt her stomach drop to the floor. This must be a bad dream. It had to be. There was no way that this was *actually* happening to her. Stuff like this never happened in real life.

"Oh god," Mack breathed out, barely feeling Beth squeezing and tugging on her arm. "Oh...god."

"Mackenzie Gomez," Principal Berkley repeated.

All eyes were on her, including Veronica's—round like saucers. The gym had gone weirdly quiet and Mack swore she could hear herself breathe.

"That's you," Beth said before frowning. "Actually...is that your full name? Mackenzie? I thought I heard your dad call you Mackerel."

"Mackenzie, can you please come up here?" the principal said a little desperately.

Mack grabbed the cup from Lila's hand and quickly downed the contents, the punch burning the back of her throat and warming her stomach. She shoved the empty cup back at Lila as she looked back up at the stage. She felt a small push on the small of her back, Beth squeezing her hand one last time as her legs moved seemingly on their own accord toward the stage. She licked her lips, mouth suddenly dry, mind racing. *Don't trip. Don't trip. Don't* fucking *trip.*

Standing on the stage, she looked at the principal, who looked just as confused as he put the sash and crown on her head. She turned to look at the audience, a sea of students staring back at her. The spotlight was hot and she was sure she was sweating through her suit shirt.

Mack's eyes caught Veronica's and she shook her head. "I don't know what's happening," Mack whispered.

Suddenly, someone started clapping and she heard Lila cheering for her, Beth joining shortly afterward. There was a smattering of applause and she could hear the principal say something, but everything sounded like she was underwater. She could feel the hot press of embarrassed years behind her eyes as she just waited for the moment to be over, but each second dragged like hours.

She felt someone grab her hand and her instinct was to yank it away, especially when she saw it was Veronica. Her eyes widened as she looked at her and Veronica offered a small smile, leading her off the stage to the middle of the dance floor that had cleared out.

"Just dance with me," Veronica said, putting Mack's hands on her waist and her own around Mack's neck. "Okay? Ignore everyone else."

"What the hell is happening?" Mack whispered as they began to sway to a slow song that Mack couldn't hear over the sound of blood rushing through her ears. "I promise I didn't do this on purpose—"

"I know," Veronica said with a stiff smile. "Is this ideal? No. Because you look like you're going to barf all over me. Which... don't, by the way. But just try and relax okay? I know you didn't do this on purpose."

Mack shook her head. "It's just— I'm sorry I—"

"I know," Veronica said. She rolled her eyes but her smile made Mack relax a little. "I get it. Plus, it was actually a sweet way to ask someone to prom. I've had a lot of bad promposals. I'm sorry I didn't stand up for you."

"It's fine. I never expected you to. I get it. It's high school and you're popular with a popular boyfriend."

Veronica shook Mack a little bit. "No. You made me realize there's more to life than that. I applied to Harvard and I'm on the waitlist, but that's further than I was before."

Mack smiled genuinely for the first time since her name was called. "I'm glad. That'll be good for you."

"We'll see," Veronica said with the hint of a blush.

"Hello!" Someone practically yelled over the microphone. Mack looked up and saw Suzan standing on the stage with a manic smile on her face. "Doesn't anyone see what I see? Veronica is a total lezzie!"

Dread overcame Mack, and she stepped away from Veronica, but Veronica stopped her, tightening her arms around Mack's neck.

"Don't," she whispered even as Mack shook her head.

"She's a big ole dyke! Just like Mack!" Suzan yelled, pointing at the two of them as whispers started to break out around them. "She's not fit to lead the cheer squad to Nationals next weekend—"

"Are you kidding me?" Mack blurted louder than she expected. "This is some serious teen movie bullshit!" Anger bloomed in her chest as she looked at Suzan. "Have you watched too many movies in your life?" Mack asked, frustration leaking through in her voice. "This isn't supposed to be a real-life thing. I'm guessing you rigged this shit so I would win?"

Suzan's face was red and blotchy, hands in fists at her sides as she stared down Mack. Her mouth was thin as she spoke again. "I don't know what you're talking about."

"Bullshit," Mack said, earning a gasp from a few teachers standing by. Chad came out of the crowd, grabbed Veronica's arm.

"What is going on here?" he hissed to her. "Is it true? Are you gay?"

Veronica scoffed and pulled her arm away from Chad. "Are you serious right now?"

The principal pushed Suzan away from the mic. "I don't know what's going on here, but everyone needs to remain calm."

Veronica dropped her arms from Mack's neck and took a step towards Suzan and the stage, fury apparent on her face. "You know what. So what if I was gay? Who cares? Leave Mack alone. She's never done anything to any of you, and you should all be ashamed for making her feel bad for who she is! She's been way nicer to me and more encouraging than any of my boyfriends ever have been, and you should all be thrilled if she even decided to talk to you."

Mack blinked herself out of her shock long enough to shake her head and lean a little into the microphone. "I'm not...all that."

Lila interrupted to pump her fist in the air and yell, "Yeah!"

The rest of the auditorium was in a stunned silence as they looked between Mack, Suzan and Veronica. Chad looked like a bull who had run ten miles, chest heaving and nostrils flaring. There was a tug on her hand and she looked over to see Beth who looked more confused than anything.

The principal cleared his throat into the microphone to get everyone's attention again. "I would like to remind you all that any sort of same-sex romantic relationship is strictly prohibited in the student handbook."

Mack felt her entire body chill again. She was definitely going to be sick now.

"Any student found to be participating in homosexual behavior *will* be dealt with and expelled. So, Mackenzie, please speak with me first thing Monday."

"Fuck," Mack breathed. She felt a squeeze to her hand before Beth shouted.

"I'm gay too!" Beth said, arm raised and a proud smile on her face. "You'll have to talk to me too, Principal Berkley."

"And me!" Lila said, stepping up next to Mack, taking her other hand. Mack looked at her best friend and smiled, tears in the corners of her eyes.

"You don't have to—"

"I do," Lila whispered, squeezing her hand again. "Ride or die. Remember?"

Principal Berkley had pulled a small notebook and pen from the inside of his blazer and was furiously writing down names.

"They can't expel all of us," Beth said.

"And me!" Veronica said, hand high and smile wide. "I'm gay!"

Suzan fist pumped in triumph. "I knew it!"

"And me!" another student said, stepping forward with their hand raised.

"And me!"

"I'm gay too!"

"Me too!"

Principal Berkley looked like he nearly strained his neck with how quickly he kept looking up and down from his notebook as more hands flew into the air.

Even Ms. Inklebam threw her hand up in the air. "Me too! I am also gay!"

Soon it was a chorus of students raising their hands, all claiming to be gay. Principal Berkley looked around confused, face getting redder with each hand that went into the air. With a final huff, he threw his notebook over his shoulder and stormed off the stage. Mack felt two sets of arms close around her, Beth on one side and Lila on the other. Only then did she let the tears of relief leak from her eyes.

"This will be addressed on Monday!" Principal Berkeley bellowed from somewhere deep in the auditorium. Suzan stalked off the stage, face redder than Mack thought humanly possible. The music started again and everyone cheered, going back to their dancing.

"I love you guys," Mack said, voice hoarse. "Fuck you both for making me cry."

"Love you too, dumbass," Lila said, kissing Mack's cheek. "Even if it didn't work out between us."

Mack jokingly pushed Lila away, wiping away her tears and putting her arm over Beth's shoulders. "You're the worst."

"Hey," Veronica said, taking a step closer to Mack and smiling brightly. "If anyone else bothers you, let me know. Okay?"

Mack nodded. "Thank you."

Veronica shrugged. "Think of it as an apology."

Mack smiled and Veronica winked at her before she turned away and disappeared into the crowd of students. Chad had gone somewhere, probably to affirm his masculinity. Lila was dancing again and Mack just stayed standing there with Beth, hugging her from the side.

"You're very brave," Beth said, kissing Mack's cheek.

"Nah," Mack said softly, turning and kissing the end of Beth's nose so that she giggled. "I'm just…doin' my thing."

Beth hummed. "Well, can you do your thing on the dance floor?" she asked, swaying her hips a little. "And then maybe later you can do your thing in the back of your car? With me?"

Mack felt heat rise in her face before it stretched into a grin. "It would be my pleasure."

Mack leaned forward and kissed Beth straight on the lips, not caring anymore who was watching.

Bella Books, Inc.

Women. Books. Even Better Together.

P.O. Box 10543
Tallahassee, FL 32302

Phone: 800-729-4992
www.bellabooks.com

MAY 1 7 2021

CPSIA information can be obtained
at www.ICGtesting.com
Printed in the USA
LVHW012241020320
648764LV00002B/3

9 781642 471151